A Candlelight Ecstasy Romance™

SHE HAD NO DESIRE TO ESCAPE . . .

She felt too gloriously alive, all her senses aroused to total receptiveness. Fascinated by the contours of taut rippling muscles, she traced them tentatively, then cupped his neck in trembling hands. Her fingers tangled compulsively in the crisp clean hair brushing his nape and she pressed closer to him.

Nick's free hand was moving over her back, arching her to him, his fingertips exploring the delicate bone structure and warm firm flesh, sending tremors of delight feathering up and down her spine. Every sensitized nerve ending conveyed his message of passion. . . .

PASSION'S PRICE

Donna Kimel Vitek

A CANDLELIGHT ECSTASY ROMANCE™

Published by
Dell Publishing Co., Inc.
1 Dag Hammarskjold Plaza
New York, New York 10017

ISBN: 0-440-17036-2

Printed in the United States of America

First printing—January 1983

To Our Readers:

We have been delighted with your enthusiastic response to Candlelight Ecstasy Romances™, and we thank you for the interest you have shown in this exciting series.

In the upcoming months we will continue to present the distinctive sensuous love stories you have come to expect only from Ecstasy. We look forward to bringing you many more books from your favorite authors and also the very finest work from new authors of contemporary romantic fiction.

As always, we are striving to present the unique, absorbing love stories that you enjoy most—books that are more than ordinary romance.

Your suggestions and comments are always welcome. Please write to us at the address below.

Sincerely,

The Editors
Candlelight Romances
1 Dag Hammarskjold Plaza
New York, New York 10017

CHAPTER ONE

Laine Winthrop slid her stockinged feet across the plush carpeting beneath her desk and sighed with relief. Relaxing back in her chair, she ran one hand lightly over her short cap of golden hair, then tugged one strand of the feathery sweep that fell to one side across her forehead. For a long thoughtful moment she gazed out the window at twin magnolia trees adorned with huge white flowers. Native to Georgia, not the cultivated variety, these two trees burst forth in spring with large glossy green leaves that further accentuated the loveliness of the creamy blossoms that bloomed later. A light breeze drifted through the office window, and Laine appreciatively inhaled the heady lemony fragrance that accompanied it. A pleasant drowsiness stole over her, but before she could nestle down more comfortably in her chair, her door was opened. The tall auburn-haired woman who stepped into the room grinned broadly.

"Liberated at last, I see," Marge Simmons drawled, strolling toward the desk. "Free of the formidable Mrs. Wainwright and of your shoes. It hasn't exactly been a fun day, has it?"

Wry amusement sparkled in Laine's wide blue eyes as she shook her head. "No, I have to admit it hasn't been one of my best. Hopefully, you're not going to make it worse by firing me for kicking off my shoes."

7

"Not likely. You're the best assistant director I've ever had, so I plan on keeping you, shoes or no shoes. And frankly, I think your father was wrong to insist you dress up in a suit and highheel pumps simply because Marian Wainwright decided to conduct an inspection. Even if she is a member of the board of trustees, she should know you're not just an administrator here. You're actively involved with the children, and you just can't wear your Sunday best to deal with nursery school and kindergarten kids."

"You know my father," Laine answered, wrinkling her nose while lifting her shoulders in a slight shrug. "As the daughter of a college president, I *must* always look impeccably respectable. 'Professional and above reproach' were his exact words I think," Laine quoted, her voice dropping two octaves as she imitated her father's somber tone.

Settling down on the corner of Laine's desk, Marge smiled wickedly. "Why don't we invite him over for a visit? After his three-piece suit has been decorated with fingerpaints, I don't think he'll ever insist you dress up for Mrs. Wainwright again." Her gaze drifted downward. "Or show him that. I see one of our little charges gave you something to remember him by."

Laughing softly, Laine glanced down at the small handprint gracing her white linen skirt just above her right knee. "Oatmeal cookie—should wash out pretty easily. And speaking of our charges, I'd better go check on mine. Mary Lou Baker's got them now, and she can't always control them."

Marge frowned. "What kind of evaluation will you give her then? If she can't maintain discipline . . ."

"She's improved since the term began. And besides, she's only a sophomore. Most people wait until their junior year to come into this program," Laine explained as she retrieved her black kid pumps from beneath her desk.

"Actually, Mary Lou's gaining more confidence every day, and since she has a natural ability to make learning fun, I think she can become a fine teacher."

"A rare breed—those with natural ability," Marge commented, then frowned as the younger woman slipped on her shoes with a slight wince. "Look, why don't you go home now. It's nearly five o'clock anyway, and on Fridays people usually pick up their children before six. I can even look in on Mary Lou for you."

For a moment Laine was tempted to accept the offer, but at last she shook her head. "No, that's okay. I'll just stay. You . . ."

"For heaven's sake, go home before your feet fall off," Marge interrupted firmly. "You deserve an hour off anyway. Besides," she added, patting the stack of folders atop the desk, "you have your work cut out for you this weekend. Mary Lou and all your other student assistants to evaluate. And grades have to be posted by Monday."

"Sometimes I think it would be very nice to average a row of test scores and determine grades solely by that," Laine commented wryly. "As it is, though, I'm sure you're right. I'll spend all weekend going over their weekly evaluations. It's the only way to really grade them fairly."

"Then go home and get started," Marge commanded, lifting the student folders and thrusting them into Laine's arms. "And soak your feet for an hour or so."

"You talked me into it," Laine agreed with a grimace. "My arches are beginning to ache a little."

"Be off with you then, while I go rescue Mary Lou," Marge quipped before walking briskly from the small office.

Within minutes, Laine was on her way across campus. Because her feet did hurt, she strolled at a casual unhurried pace along the cobbled sidewalks. A gentle cooling breeze played with wisps of her hair and rustled the thick shiny leaves of the magnolias. Snow white camellia blossoms studded dark green foliage and provided a festive touch to the ivy-covered brick buildings that surrounded the grassy commons. Latham College was an old school, steeped in tradition. Laine often wondered if anything here had ever changed since Andrew Latham had opened the doors way back in the 1840s. The school's appearance certainly hadn't altered in her lifetime, but she found the perpetual sameness comforting. Latham was home, and she had no desire to leave, despite living with a father who rarely if ever showed her affection. Though he had never said he loved her, she tried to assume he did, at least in his own way. Yet she knew she was a disappointment to him; that was a fact of life she had accepted for fourteen years—ever since her mother had died when she was ten.

Thornton Winthrop had wanted his second child to be a son. Laine's gender might not have mattered so much to him had she proved to be an exceptional little girl, but she hadn't been blessed with any extraordinary talents. Before her marriage, Laine's mother had been an acclaimed concert pianist, but her second daughter didn't inherit her musical genius nor her exquisite loveliness. It was Laine's sister, Regina, older by five years, who was the child of rare beauty and the beneficiary of almost all their father's attention. Laine's loving, generous nature hadn't seemed to impress Thornton Winthrop very much.

Despite that, Laine's childhood had been happy. Her mother loved her dearly and instilled in her a sense of self-worth no amount of a father's inattention could diminish. After her mother died, ten-year-old Laine had felt somewhat lost and alone for a time, but an inherent joyousness had triumphed, enabling her to accept Thornton's lack of affection with little more than a vague sense of disappointment.

Still, even now that she was an adult, Laine occasionally

regretted she couldn't be closer to her father. It would be nice to know he was proud of her, but she couldn't think how she could possibly do more to try to please him. After all, she was already making a success of her chosen career. She had many friends and was an attractive young woman. Her warm blue eyes, soft blond hair, and slight yet shapely body had caught the glances of many young men even if she couldn't compete with Regina's stunning statuesque beauty. It wasn't her fault she didn't have her sister's natural platinum hair and bewitching violet eyes. She was what she was and she did the best she could, she told herself as she continued across the campus's main square; then she temporarily pushed all thoughts about her father to the back of her mind.

After passing the bookstore and waving to a friend who manned the counter by the window, Laine lifted her face to the warming rays of the late May sun. This was one of her favorite times of year. Though Latham College was located only five miles inland from the Atlantic, the campus was surrounded by pine forests, which helped alleviate some of summer's excessive heat. Situated south of Savannah and ten miles north of Brunswick, the village of Latham was so tiny it couldn't even qualify as a small town; its quiet charm and peacefulness were the qualities that appealed most to Laine.

Turning down the lane that was Faculty Row, she smiled at the ancient sea oaks, dripping with Spanish moss, that lined the street. She couldn't imagine willingly leaving this place forever, as Regina had done seven years ago, when the bright lights of big cities had lured her away. It was ironic that Thornton Winthrop's favorite daughter didn't share his love for Latham, but Laine knew he could forgive Regina anything, even that particular disloyalty. Pausing for a moment to inhale the sweet fragrance of the white roses growing at the edge of Dean

11

Jacobs's yard, Laine smiled ruefully. Despite her father's ability to ignore that one fairly serious failure of Regina's, she suspected that his love for Latham College surpassed even his adoration of her elder sister. Only their mother had come before his position here, and since her death he had immersed himself in his work, determined to make Latham the best small college in Georgia. His dedication bordered on obsession.

Though Laine's dedication was far less intense, she did appreciate the graciousness of life on a college campus and she enjoyed living in the house her mother had loved so well. Thornton Winthrop's residence befitted his position as college president; situated at the end of a cul-de-sac at the peak of a gently rolling hill, it presided in a queenly manner over the homes of the most prestigious members of faculty and staff. Traditional wrought-iron filigrees along the boundaries of the lower veranda and the second-story balcony were like delicate etching against the background of cream stucco walls. Scattered cedars shaded much of the lawn, but sunlit flower beds—tended long ago by Laine's mother—bordered the flagstone walkway. Thornton tended them now, and as Laine reached the veranda she noticed that the blue southern stars by the stairs were blooming a bit early this year.

After checking that the potted fern by the doorway wasn't in need of water, Laine limped into the house. The walk home hadn't helped her feet, so she immediately kicked off her shoes and hobbled across the foyer to the staircase. She put the student folders down on the second step and sank down on the first to begin massaging her arches. She breathed soft contented sighs as the muscles started relaxing. Warmth tingled in her toes while her fingers continued the soothing massage. Sunlight reflected from the crystal chandelier danced and sparkled on the polished hardwood floor. The house was quiet. Laine felt a sudden rush of gladness because her father wasn't there. Although she loved him, he often seemed so completely unapproachable that she felt uneasy in his presence. She had even considered leaving home to move into one of the tiny faculty apartments two streets away, but there was a waiting list of people who wanted one. And besides, if she moved out, her father would have to hire a housekeeper to take care of him. So she stayed, accepted his silences, and was grateful for times like this when she could truly relax because she had the house to herself.

Her solitude was abruptly and rudely interrupted when the doorchimes echoed in the foyer. "Damn," she muttered. With extreme reluctance, she eased her sore feet back into her shoes and walked gingerly across the foyer to open the door.

A tall dark-haired man in his midthirties was leaning on one hand against the doorjamb, but he straightened immediately when Laine appeared on the threshold. "That was fast. Maybe you were expecting someone else," he commented, surveying her from head to toe with one swift appraising glance. Then jade green eyes met hers directly. "I want to see Thornton Winthrop. Is he in?"

"No, he isn't. I'm sorry," Laine said, curiously surveying him too, sure she had never seen him around campus before. She would have remembered him, she was certain, because he was highly noticeable, a truly attractive man. The subtly muscular contours of his long hard body exuded virility and those piercing eyes were set in a classically Roman face. His finely chiseled features suggested a certain ruthlessness, yet . . . there was something else, a quality Laine couldn't name. Giving up on trying to make an instant analysis, she smiled politely at him. "My father's usually still in his office this time of day. If you'd like to try to find him there . . ."

13

The man shook his head. "No, I'll just wait here for him. You don't mind if I come in?"

His assured commanding tone caught Laine off guard for a second, but she recovered in time to plant herself firmly in the doorway, an incongruously slight figure facing someone of such obviously superior strength as if she actually believed she could prevent his entering. "I'm afraid I do mind," she challenged hastily. "I don't even know your name. Just who are you anyway?"

"Nicolas Brannon. Maybe my uncle's mentioned me," he said, his voice vibrantly deep and melodious though his words were crisp. When he noticed the questioning frown that knitted Laine's forehead, he elaborated. "My uncle is Phillip Winston. I believe that name should ring a bell on this campus."

"Of course his name rings a bell. Phillip Winston is highly respected here at Latham," Laine said, though the uncertain frown still lingered on her brow. "But I can't say I recall Mr. Winston ever mentioning a nephew."

"Maybe he hasn't mentioned me then," Nick Brannon conceded with an easy unconcerned smile. "Uncle Phillip probably does tend to lose himself in memories of his college days when he visits here."

"That's true," Laine said, her frown fading. "And for some reason, Mr. Brannon, your name does sound familiar to me."

"Excellent. Now do you think it's safe to let me in?" he asked, a hint of amusement gentling his tone. He moved toward Laine. "Or are you going to make me wait here on the veranda until your father comes home?"

"Certainly not. Do come in, please." Stepping back from the doorway, she extended one arm, then felt as if the space in the foyer diminished when Nick Brannon entered. Tilting her head back, she attempted a nonchalant smile and, succeeding, graciously directed him into the

14

living room. "Please sit down. Make yourself comfortable."

He did. Taking a seat, he loosened his tie and unfastened his collar button. With a confident unapologetic smile at Laine, he draped one arm across the back of the blue brocade sofa.

"Could I get you a drink?" Laine asked, and when he declined, she settled herself in the chair opposite him. As he continued to observe her in silence, she at last added rather lamely, "My father should be home soon, Mr. Brannon."

"Nick is sufficient, *Miss* Winthrop. I assume it is Miss and I also assume you have a first name. Perhaps you should tell me what it is, since I plan to spend a few days here and it might come in handy to know what to call you."

His unabashed straightforwardness was irresistibly charming and she had to smile at him. "I'm Laine Winthrop, and I'm very pleased to meet you, Mr. Bran— Nick."

"The pleasure's all mine." Allowing a longer lingering gaze to drift over her, he leaned forward, resting his elbows on his knees. "Do you go to school here, Laine? Or are you just home for the summer?"

"I'm one of the faculty here," she said simply, working to control her amusement as she watched a look of surprise register on his face. For some reason it felt very good to catch this self-assured man off guard.

"And do you simply look young for your age or are you one of those geniuses who finish college at fifteen or sixteen?"

Laine laughed. "With that kind of lead I'd be a fool to deny a certain . . . above-average intelligence. But I did finish college at the usual pace. I'm just older than I look."

"Someday I'm sure you'll consider that an asset," he

countered wryly, sitting back again to stretch his long legs out before him. "So what do you teach?"

"I teach teachers how to teach, actually. I'm assistant director of the nursery school–kindergarten we've opened on campus. It allows us to give the students who hope to teach someday the chance to deal with a classroom of children. Experience always helps," she continued, enthusiasm sparkling in her blue eyes. "Did you realize Latham used to be exclusively a teachers' college? That's no longer true, but many of our students are planning careers in education."

Nick Brannon nodded. "You sound happy with your work." Flicking back the sides of his gray pinstriped suit coat, he regarded her intently. "And is your social life just as satisfying, I wonder?"

"Well, I . . ."

"Or do you have one? Maybe you're one of those women who want to make a career your entire existence?"

"I'd never want to live just for a career," she stated honestly.

"Isn't life on a small campus like this fairly restrictive?"

"And isn't this conversation getting a little personal?" she shot back. She stared at him, wondering what in the world had brought on this inquisition. Then recognition dawned with sudden clarity and she smiled. "Of course, you're *that* Nick Brannon—the attorney. I knew the name sounded familiar, but I couldn't place it until you started grilling me."

Nick's deep rumble of answering laughter was directed at himself. "I guess I was grilling you, wasn't I? Sorry, but I was in court in Savannah all day and sometimes I bring my courtroom manner out with me. Occupational hazard."

"I can see that it would be," Laine said dryly.

He laughed.

"Now, I understand how you win most of your cases," she added. "I've read about some of them in the newspaper. I was convinced that doctor in Phoenix would be convicted of murdering his wife, although I had an instinctive feeling he wasn't guilty, despite the evidence. I was so relieved when you got him acquitted."

"So was he," Nick responded flatly. "And so was I. Defense attorneys who lose cases don't attract many new clients."

"I bet not," Laine agreed, animation brightening her delicate facial features. "Your work must be terribly exciting. It seems as if you always get involved in highly publicized trials."

A secretive smile lifted the corners of Nick's firmly carved mouth. "Publicity's what you make of it, and sometimes I go out of my way to encourage it to gain sympathy for my clients. Though it shouldn't, it can occasionally mean the difference between conviction and acquittal."

"Could you tell me about some of your cases that are closed now?" Laine asked, genuinely interested. "How have you managed to win almost all the ones I've read about during the past two or three years?"

Lifting one hand in protest, he shook his head. "Practicing law isn't what it seems to be on television. If you're imagining I'm some sort of Perry Mason, don't. I'm not. I don't win all my cases. I lose some too—too many to suit me—and some losses are more than just frustrating. They're tragic."

For the next twenty minutes or so, Nick told Laine about some of his defeats, lingering longest on his account about a young man wrongly convicted of armed robbery. Nick had no doubts about his innocence, but unfortunately circumstantial evidence had been damning; the man had been swiftly convicted in his first trial, then once again on appeal. Afterwards, Nick had been unable to get any higher court to hear the case, and there was nowhere to go from there. So the man was still in prison for a crime he didn't commit. Listening to Nick relate this story, watching him, Laine could easily see that though he might be capable of ruthlessness, he was was also capable of caring. A muscle ticked in his tightened jaw when he spoke of the injustice done to his client. There was an unyielding edge to his impassioned tone, and the hard relentless expression on his sun-browned face suggested he would fight to the last breath to prevent such a travesty of justice from occurring again.

"Isn't there anything else you can do?" Laine asked softly when he finished speaking. "Surely there's something?"

A grim smile hardened his mouth. "Pertinent new evidence that we didn't have at the trial could win an appeal. But new evidence isn't easy to find. It doesn't just crop up conveniently."

"So your client just sits in prison for something he didn't do."

"That's what it amounts to, until he's eligible for parole."

"How's he taking it? I mean, he must be very bitter."

Some of the tension seemed to leave Nick. His taut features relaxed and some warmth returned to his eyes as they sought Laine's. "That's the only positive note to this entire case—he's not bitter, at least not very. He made himself accept the situation and he's trying to make the best of it. He's taking college courses through an inmate program and he swears he'll never be in trouble with the law again. He had a record of petty offenses before the armed robbery charge and that was one of the reasons he seemed likely to be guilty. That's what one of the jurors told me after the verdict."

18

Nibbling her lower lip, Laine nodded thoughtfully. "Well, at least he's thinking about his future. I guess a little something came out of the whole wretched mess."

"At this point, that's the only way to look at it. But . . ."

Laine nodded again when Nick left his statement unfinished. "You're right. Real attorneys don't have it as easy as the ones on TV."

"Not quite," he retorted wryly, then glanced at his wristwatch.

Prompted to look at her own, Laine was surprised to discover it was already a few minutes past six. During her conversation with Nick, time had passed more quickly than she had imagined, but now she realized her father was usually home earlier than this. A slight frown marked her smooth brow. "Father's a little late, but he should be here soon. Would you care for a drink while you wait?"

This time Nick didn't decline, and as she walked across the white area rug to the bar at the side of the room, she sensed he was watching her. She suddenly became far too aware of her own movements, and a strange sensation dragged at her stomach. Though she was not unaccustomed to being observed by men, this man was different. There was a disturbing intensity about him, as if ardent emotions were held in check just beneath the surface, and she shivered to think what might happen if those emotions were given free rein. Nick Brannon was definitely not a man to be taken lightly, and as she poured his Scotch and water, then her own white wine, she began to wonder why he had come to see her father.

A moment later, she asked him. When the lips of his long brown fingers grazed hers as she handed him his drink, she felt the oddest sense of danger and shied away. Taking a quick step back from him, she blurted out, "You never said why you're here to see my father." Then she added, in a light, almost flip, tone, "He doesn't need a criminal attorney, does he?" The thought of the upright, ever moral Thornton Winthrop running afoul of the law was almost laughable.

"Not that I'm aware of," Nick replied, his eyes hooded by thick brown lashes as he looked at her over the rim of the glass he held to his lips. "I'm here about the grant."

"Grant?"

"Yes, the million-dollar grant my uncle gives annually to Latham College. Of course, you know about that?"

"Sure, but . . . what about it?"

Nick held her puzzled gaze. "My uncle has suffered a series of small strokes. Perhaps you haven't heard. He's recovering now but isn't well enough to handle his own affairs. He's given me power of attorney to act for him."

Laine restlessly shifted her still sore feet. "And?"

"And I thought I'd come see how the money's been spent in the past."

"Your uncle's never thought it necessary to do that."

"My uncle's a brilliant businessman, but he's amazingly sentimental when it comes to his old alma mater," Nick explained calmly. "Recently, I convinced him it might not be wise to go on automatically giving the grant. He's never stipulated how past grants were to be spent, so I'm here to find out how they were. And I'll want to know specifically where the money will go if the grant's given this year."

"If?" Laine's voice was somewhat strained. Her heart thudded heavily with sudden dread as she sank down on her chair, nearly spilling wine from her glass in the process. Unable to look at Nick, she sipped her wine. "What exactly do you mean by 'if?'" she said with a casualness she certainly did not feel. "Are you saying that Latham might not be awarded the grant this year?"

Nick didn't answer for so long that Laine was finally

forced to look up at him. When she did, he was stroking his cheek with one finger, as if he were weighing his response. "Yes, I guess that's exactly what I'm saying," he said at last, watching her closely with no definable expression whatsoever on his lean rugged face. "There is a possibility Latham won't be awarded the grant this year."

Laine groaned inwardly, lowering her head so the thick fringe of her lashes hid the disappointment mirrored in her eyes. Her father would be positively livid when he heard about this turn of events. And he was already practically overcome with worry. Nick Brannon could be relentless; intuition made her certain of that fact. Once he made a decision he thought was right, he wouldn't change his mind. So if he decided Latham College didn't deserve the grant, the grant wouldn't be given.

CHAPTER TWO

Laine took a deep nerve-steadying breath. Her troubled blue eyes met the untroubled jade of his. "Maybe you don't understand what a million dollars means to a small college like Latham," she said at last. "What that amount of money can do . . . well, you just must not understand."

"That's why I'm here—to discover exactly what the money does mean to the college." Nick shrugged. "I don't think it's unreasonable for the contributor of a million dollars a year to want to know how the money's being spent, even if the grants are given with no strings attached. Do you think it's unreasonable?"

"Well, no," Laine conceded. Unconsciously, she ran her fingers through her golden hair, slightly tousling the silken strands that swept across her forehead. She began to twirl one tendril round and round one finger until she realized Nick was watching her closely. Her right hand dropped back down to the chair's armrest. "I can understand your uncle wanting to know what's being done with the grants. What I don't understand is that he's never seemed the least bit curious before. What's the difference this year?"

Nick shrugged again. "I told you it was my idea. Since I'm handling his affairs at the moment, I'm doing a thorough job of it. I'm always very thorough."

"I'm sure of it. Of course, Latham College is not exactly

like one of your criminal cases," she said slowly, her words laced with a subtly cutting edge.

One corner of Nick's mouth lifted in a sardonic smile. "You're acting rather defensive about this, Laine."

"Perhaps it's because you act as if you suspect someone of something," she shot back indignantly, color heightening to a deep rose tint in her cheeks. "Why have you come to see my father? Why didn't you meet with the board of trustees? My father's not solely responsible for handling those grants you know. The board has a great deal to do with spending your uncle's money. Why single my father out? He loves Latham College, and he's an honest man. If you're insinuating that he misuses funds, you . . ."

"I'm not insinuating anything," Nick interrupted tersely. A hint of impatience flickered across his face as he glared at her. "If I thought the grants had been misused, I'd have come here with accountants to go over the books. Your defense of your father is admirable but totally unnecessary, unless you know something I don't know yet. Do you?"

"Of course not," Laine answered crisply, striving to maintain that disturbing eye contact with him. "But why begin your inquiry with my father? Surely the board . . ."

"I shy away from trustee boards whenever possible; three fourths of the members must attend meetings in their sleep. They seem to know very little about practicalities. But men in your father's position do more than make broad sweeping decisions. They have to keep up with the details. I'm here to see your father simply because he probably knows more about Latham College than anyone else."

"That's true. But it's the board that makes the final decisions."

"The board be damned," was Nick's succinct reply,

23

dismissing the entire governing body of the college with a careless flick of one large tan hand. "Does that express my lack of confidence in them clearly enough for you?"

"You've made yourself quite clear," Laine replied, the sudden smile that danced on her generously curved lips becoming soft laughter. "You know, you sounded just like my father when you said 'The board be damned.' I don't think a week goes by that he doesn't make that same assessment."

"Then we'll have something in common when we meet," Nick said dryly before taking another sip of his drink. "My visit here might turn out to be less of an ordeal than you seem to think it's going to be."

Laine's smile wavered slightly, became more apologetic than amused. She felt something of a fool for misconstruing his motive for coming here. Yet there was something about his manner that had put her on the defensive. "You did act as if you had some sort of suspicions about something," she said after a moment. "Anyway, that's the impression I got."

"The price I pay for being a lawyer," he drawled, his smile etching attractive indentations into his cheeks beside his mouth. "We attorneys *are* a suspicious lot, by nature. Maybe it's all the wild stories we've had to listen to. We soon learn it's usually wise to have some initial doubts."

"You needn't doubt my father's honesty. He's an honorable man."

"I'm sure he is."

"You don't sound sure," Laine protested softly, wide eyes searching his face. "You still sound as if you're suspicious."

Nick leaned forward toward her. "Laine, look, I can't be sure what kind of man your father is until I've met him, can I? I'm not assuming the worst of him, I assure you,

24

but I'll reserve judgment until I've met him. Then I'll decide for myself what kind of man I think he is."

Laine sniffed. "You certainly don't give people the benefit of the doubt, do you?"

"And are you such a trusting little soul, Laine?" he asked, his voice a husky whisper, his smile teasingly suggestive. His narrowed gaze roved over her with lingering slowness as he thoughtfully stroked the clear line of his jaw with one forefinger. "Hmm. I'll be sure to remember that. You're an extremely attractive young woman. If you're all *that* trusting, I just might extend my visit here."

"Oh, I'll readily admit to being trusting of mankind in general. It's men in *particular* I'm wary of, Mr. Brannon," she retorted with a pert grin.

Nick answered her barb with a burst of laughter, a deep, utterly masculine sound that made her feel unaccountably warm inside. He looked boldly into her eyes, his own eyes sparkling with amusement . . . and something more; some indefinable challenge that both excited her and awakened an instinctive warning to proceed cautiously with this man.

She felt a vague disappointment when she heard her father coming into the house. Nick Brannon was an intriguing man, and she would have preferred to have him to herself for a little while longer. But maybe it was best that their moment of intimacy was cut short. He might well prove hard to handle. He was far too attractive, she thought, and though she had the last word this time around, she'd be fooling herself to believe she could ever win the war of words with him. He undoubtedly deserved his reputation for being exceptionally adept at confusing a witness. In the short space of one hour, he had caused her to leap to her father's defense though he needed no defense. Now he practically had her blushing like an adolescent, and her usual cool composure seemed to be developing a few disturbing cracks. If any other man had tried flirting with her so outrageously, she would have simply dismissed him with a good-natured laugh or a comment designed to put him in his place. But Nick Brannon couldn't be so easily dismissed. Even as Laine's father walked into the living room, Nick was still watching her, giving her that teasing, gently taunting, smile.

Striving to ignore its intimations, she responded with a blithe smile of her own, then transferred it to her father. When he showed no inclination to return it, she realized that Nick's nearness to her as he leaned forward might be giving Thornton the impression that he was interrupting a tête-à-tête. She hastily introduced the two men.

To his credit, Thornton showed no discernible reaction when Nick promptly explained his visit to the Latham campus. Instead, Laine's father greeted the younger man cordially, without the undue obsequious effervescence that would have proved he was ill at ease. Waving Nick back into his seat after they shook hands, he proceeded to the bar to pour himself a drink, all the while keeping up polite small talk. A tall dignified man with a thick silvery mane of hair, Thornton Winthrop was at fifty-eight an extremely handsome man. Many of the women members of the faculty and staff would have been overjoyed to have received an interested glance from him, but to Laine's knowledge he had never looked seriously at another woman since her mother's death. Because of that, Laine sometimes felt almost sorry for him, but as she watched him at the bar, acting for all the world as though a million-dollar grant was of little significance, he seemed too impressive to ever warrant pity. There was no denying he was handling Nick Brannon's surprise visit much better than she had. But then, he had years of experience with benefactors whereas she was only a novice.

For the next few minutes, while Thornton stood casual-

26

ly beside the concert grand piano that had been his wife's and inquired about the health of Nick's uncle, Laine merely listened; then she quietly excused herself. As she moved to return her wine glass to the bar, her father flicked a cursory glance in her direction.

"You seem to have a palm print on your skirt, Laine," he announced, his cool tone clearly stating that he didn't appreciate untidiness when they had such an important guest. She didn't believe he ever deliberately meant to wound her with his criticisms, but he could be terribly insensitive at times.

"That's what happens when you wear a white linen suit into a kindergarten class, Father," she answered flatly, not the least bit intimidated by his disapproval. After all, he was the one who had insisted she go to work overdressed today, and she was satisfied her answer had reminded him of that fact. Switching her attention from him to Nick, she smiled carelessly and uselessly brushed one hand across the smudged fabric of her skirt. "Oatmeal cookie," she explained, then added, "I'm sure you'll forgive my appearance, won't you, Nick? I didn't have time to change before you came."

"Okay, if you promise to *never* let it happen again," he quipped, making nonsense of the entire overblown matter.

Laine wrinkled her nose at him and joined him in muted amused laughter. When she walked past her father on her way to the bar, she noticed with some unbidden sense of satisfaction that he didn't particularly seem to approve of her exchange of lighthearted banter with Nick.

A moment later, after Laine had offered to freshen Nick's drink and he had declined, Thornton took a gold-framed photograph from its place of honor on the piano and handed it to the younger man. "Did Laine show you this? It's my older daughter, Regina. She looks exactly like her mother did at that same age. Lovely, isn't she?"

27

Nodding, Nick examined the platinum-haired beauty who beamed a dazzling smile up from the photograph. "Yes, she's very lovely."

"She's a model," Laine contributed as she returned from the bar to sit down again. "In New York."

"Maybe you've seen her on magazine covers," Thornton added proudly. "She's very much in demand."

Nick's darkening gaze drifted from Laine to her father, then back to her again. When she detected unmistakable understanding in the depths of his eyes, plus a hint of something akin to compassion, she was amazed at his swift perceptiveness. Though she felt some resentment toward her father for making her appear vulnerable to Nick, she managed a genuine smile.

"We're very proud of Regina," she said honestly. "But she's so busy, she hardly ever comes home. I miss her."

"I'm sure she must miss you too," Nick said softly, returning the photograph to Thornton, though his eyes never left Laine's face. "If the two of you are like my two younger sisters, you're probably very close."

"Yes, we're even closer now that we're adults," Laine told him, smiling fondly as she willingly shared a memory. "We really used to fight like cats. I thought she was far too bossy, and she considered me an aggravating little brat. During some of our louder more energetic spats, Mother used to threaten to throw us both out of the house."

"Well, Nick, you are staying for dinner this evening, aren't you?" Thornton interceded, rushing a change of subject as if he could hardly bear to hear Laine's reminiscences of happier days when his beloved wife was still alive. Yet there was not one shadow of emotion on his face as he regarded Nick inquiringly. "Laine did invite you, didn't she?"

"As a matter of fact, Father, I hadn't yet," Laine answered, giving Nick a sincerely gracious smile that reflected an inbred hospitality. "We'd love for you to stay for dinner if you wouldn't mind taking potluck. Friday is always my day off from cooking. Father usually fends for himself."

"I'm sure you can prepare an excellent meal, if you really try," Thornton said brusquely. "Even on such short notice."

"I'm not exactly a gourmet chef, Father. Let's not get Nick's hopes too high," she replied smoothly, her only sign of rebellion a slight compressing of her lips. Then she suddenly smiled. "I have a better idea than potluck anyway. I bought some very nice steaks yesterday. Why don't you bring out the charcoal, Father?" She turned to Nick. "His grilled steaks are really delicious."

Thornton had no choice except to acquiesce. He nodded his agreement, then countered with an idea of his own. "And after dinner, Nick, I'm sure you'd like a tour of the campus so you can see some of the projects your uncle's money has contributed to. Laine will show you around."

Now she was unable to protest, though she probably should have. Her father knew full well that she had all those student evaluations to finish this weekend, but she suspected he had maneuvered her into this corner deliberately anyhow. Why he should do that was a mystery she gave little thought to at that moment, however. Her mind immediately became occupied with more disturbing thoughts—when she stood, Nick's jade eyes lingered on her long shapely legs, then wandered lazily upward. Though she gave him a nonchalant smile, her heartbeat had accelerated. And when she excused herself to go up to her room to change clothes, she wondered how unwise it was even to consider going for a moonlit stroll with Nick Brannon.

Ten minutes later, after slipping into a comfortable ice

29

blue cotton shirtwaist and blessedly unconfining leather sandals, Laine felt like a new woman. She ran lightly down the stairs to the kitchen, where she sprinkled coarse salt over baking potatoes before putting them into the oven. While nibbling a carrot stick, she prepared a fresh green salad and her own blue cheese dressing and looked frequently out the window at her father and Nick on the patio. Both men had shed their jackets and ties, and Nick looked as comfortable in the outdoor setting as she imagined he would be in a courtroom. The sleeves of his white shirt were rolled up to just above his elbows, exposing cleanly muscled forearms bronzed by the sun. Wondering how his busy career allowed much time for being out of doors, Laine gently tore tender leaves of lettuce into a large wooden bowl as she watched her father start toward the outside kitchen door.

Despite the chef's apron tied round his middle, Thornton Winthrop exuded cool dignity. Back ramrod straight, he strode into the kitchen, then stopped and stared at his daughter expectantly.

"The steaks are ready," she told him. "They're in the fridge."

Silently, Thornton removed a platter from the refrigerator and quickly examined the steaks. Obviously they passed inspection, because he made no complaint, which was a relief. Particular as he was about the quality of the cuts of meat he grilled, he often preached sermons on wise buying habits if Laine presented him with steaks he considered less than perfect.

Accustomed as she was to his silences, Laine expected him to leave the kitchen without a word to her. But as she sliced cherry tomatoes in half to add to the lettuce, she noticed he paused momentarily by the door. She turned and tilted her head to one side questioningly when she found him regarding her with something like speculation.

"Brannon is obviously attracted to you, and that can work to our advantage," Thornton pronounced. Ignoring her surprise, he continued, "Show him the library addition tonight and the lab building and the student center. Money from Phillip Winston's grants went into all those projects. But more importantly, Laine, be very nice to him."

"I'm always nice to people. Mother taught me to be."

"I know what your mother taught you," he snapped, his stern patrician face exhibiting more emotion than usual. "And you know exactly what I mean when I ask you to be very nice to Brannon."

Laine tensed. "No, I'm not sure I do know. Maybe you'd better explain."

"For God's sake, don't pick now to be obstinate! You know what this grant means to Latham. And you've been out with enough young men to know how to be your most charming."

"If you expect me to throw myself at Nick Brannon, you'd better think again," she declared. "I'll go along with you in little things like overdressing occasionally for nursery school, but this is different. Even for a million-dollar grant, I refuse to chase after a man, especially a man who might very well be married. Come to think of it, I do seem to remember reading somewhere that he has a very lovely wife."

"Nonsense. He's not wearing a ring."

"Which doesn't necessarily mean he *isn't* married, Father. Many men don't wear wedding rings."

"Brannon's not married. I'm certain of that."

"I'm not."

"Well, I am, so just be very nice to him tonight," Thornton commanded before striding purposely out of the kitchen, the platter of steaks balanced on one hand.

"Impossible man," Laine muttered to herself as she

tossed the salad. Even a few minutes later, when she carried a tray of cutlery and dishes out onto the patio, she couldn't help glaring resentfully at her father, but if he noticed, he showed no sign. Then resentment was forgotten as Nick strode across the tiled patio to kindly help her spread a cloth over the round table. Though her cork-heeled sandals added to her height, the top of Laine's head still barely reached a level with Nick's shoulders. And when he moved closer to her, so close that she imagined she could feel the warmth emanating from his body, she was suddenly overcome by a sensual awareness of him. She discreetly moved away, hoping to high heaven he was married. A man like Nick Brannon was far too dangerous to be running around footloose and fancy-free. A woman could get ideas about him, disturbing ideas that shocked Laine in their erotic intensity, and she did her best to cast such insane visions right out of her mind.

She didn't totally succeed. Sitting next to Nick at table a half hour later, she became far more concerned about his knee occasionally brushing against her own than she was about the delicious steak on the plate before her. She ate, but it might as well have been sawdust she put into her mouth for all the attention she paid to it. Although she added occasionally to the dinner conversation, she was more interested in listening to Nick. No topic daunted him. He seemed to possess considerable knowledge in a variety of subjects, an attribute that impressed her more than she wanted it to. If he knew nothing except what he had gleaned from law books, he would have been boring and far less appealing. His appeal was enhanced by wit and intrinsic intelligence, and Laine's attraction to him deepened.

Perhaps her father sensed that. Without warning, he asked, "Are you married, Nick?"

"I've been told I'm not the marrying kind," the younger

man replied with an easy smile. "And I guess maybe I'm not, since I'm still a bachelor."

The sideward glance Thornton gave his daughter said "I told you so," clearly but discreetly. It was unfortunate his next statement wasn't so discreet.

"Since you plan to be here a few days, Nick, we'd be pleased to have you stay in our guest room."

Much to Laine's relief, Nick shook his head. "I appreciate the offer, but I don't want my visit to cause any inconvenience. I passed a motel about ten miles from here. Thought I'd check in there."

"No use driving back tonight though," Thornton persisted. "Check in tomorrow and stay here tonight. Our guest room is far more comfortable than motel accommodations, I'm sure. Don't you agree, Laine?"

"Of course," was the only response she could give, and she added somewhat weakly, "We'd be happy to have you stay."

"Since you insist, I will then," he replied with a smile that seemed to say he had merely been awaiting her personal invitation. "For tonight, at least."

"Excellent, excellent," Thornton intoned, hiding most of his satisfaction behind a placid expression. "And since you'll be sleeping here tonight, there'll be more time for you to tour the campus. Then when you tire of that, Laine can take you to the tavern. Many of the younger faculty members frequent it."

"I'm agreeable if Laine is," Nick said amicably, cutting his eyes in her direction. "Are you, Laine?"

"I think that would be very nice," she responded, unable to suppress a rising excitement. She really wanted to be with Nick, yet resented deeply her father's manipulation of the situation. Besides, his motive for throwing them together was so patently obvious it was embarrassing.

And Thornton wasn't finished yet. He ascended the pinnacle of indiscretion with his next suggestion. "Laine, it's just occurred to me that Nick could escort you to the faculty party tomorrow night. That will be the perfect opportunity for him to meet most of the staff."

Laine nearly choked on a sip of rosé wine. Mortification flew in crimson flags in her cheeks and finally rebellion seethed forth. "Father, really, I . . ."

"Perhaps Laine already has an escort to the party," Nick suggested casually.

"It isn't that. I'd be honored to have you escort me to the party but . . ." The slight movement of one small hand was actually an attempted apology for her father's uncharacteristic behavior. "Well, the truth is I hadn't planned on going to the party. I have to evaluate all my student assistants and have their grades posted by Monday. I hadn't planned on going out at all this weekend."

"Nonsense," Thornton snapped, casting her a warning glance. "Surely you'll have sufficient time to do the evaluations and go to the party too. And remember: all work and no play . . ."

Defiance sparked blue fire in her eyes, but she tried to smile and keep her tone light as she responded, "Has it occurred to you, Father, that Nick might not want to escort me?" Pride made her attempt to laugh teasingly. "I may be far from ideal in your estimation, but you don't have to coerce men into taking me out—not yet, anyway."

"I never allow myself to be pushed into doing something I don't want to do, Laine," Nick interceded, his voice low, his tone sincere, his darkening gaze magnetic as it captured and held her own. "And I do want to take you to the party."

"But the evaluations . . ."

"You can't work continuously," Nick firmly interrupted her protest. "I want you to go to the party with me. Please."

For an instant she hesitated, stymied by indecision. Finally, his unmistakable sincerity won her over, and she nodded. Yet her father's strange behavior was still a source of embarrassment for her and she didn't really feel at ease for the remainder of the meal.

Later, after washing dishes, Laine returned to the living room. The moment she entered, Nick stood and took the initiative. "Ready to give me the grand tour?" When she nodded, he left her father and came across the room.

Outside a moment later, in the muted glow of a yellow crescent moon, Nick's right hand curved into the small of Laine's back as they started walking toward the center of campus. His long fingers warmed her skin through the thin fabric of her dress and curious tingling sensations radiated along her spine. She stopped short and turned to face him, still very uneasy.

"I have to apologize," she blurted out. "My father would never act like this if that grant weren't so important to the college."

"I understand that; you don't have to explain or apologize," Nick assured her softly, his face unreadable in shadow. "I've been offered bribes before, but I have to admit, this is the first time anyone's ever offered his own daughter."

Stung by the truth so plainly spoken, Laine turned on one heel and attempted to start back toward the house, but Nick swiftly clasped one hand around her right wrist. He pulled her back to him. His arms came around her. Exploring hands ran over her back, then molded her slight, softly curved form against the hard wholly masculine line of his. When she gasped, a slight smile played over his sensuously carved lips.

Tense in the circle of his arms, she gazed up at him. "I

wish you hadn't said that," she chided shakily. "It was too blunt."

"But honest. Your father's hoping you'll be able to influence my decision about the grant."

The tip of Laine's tongue came out to moisten suddenly dry lips as she shook her head. "I couldn't influence you."

"Ah, don't be too sure of that."

Her breath caught. She struggled but was pressed closer as a result, so her struggles ceased. "Now listen, Nick," she protested weakly. "If you expect me to . . ."

"I don't expect anything from you . . . yet," he whispered close to her ear as her eyes widened.

And Laine had no idea whether he was teasing or being completely serious.

CHAPTER THREE

For the next hour or so, Laine became an efficient, knowledgable tour guide. Deciding Nick's provocative statement had been made jokingly, she dismissed it, relaxed, and confidently showed him around campus. Although her affection for Latham College must have been obvious to Nick, he didn't respond to it, nor did he give any indication as to whether or not he was impressed when Laine showed him the new library wing, lab building, and student center. Prompted by his noncommittal expression, she tried harder. After returning to the first floor of the two-story center, she led the way through the mingling groups of students celebrating end of exams to the bronze plaque prominently displayed on a wall near the entrance.

With a hopeful smile she gestured toward the short row of names engraved on the burnished sheet of metal. "You see, your uncle's name is listed first, as usual, because we do appreciate the fact that he is Latham's most generous benefactor."

Nick merely nodded, then glanced around at the loudly chattering groups of students. Soon his attention was riveted for a long still moment on a daring coed who roller-skated at breakneck speed across the tiled lobby to the cheers of friends watching from the mezzanine. When a campus security guard quickly halted the daredevil's progress and made her remove her skates, Nick looked back down at Laine with an expectant quirk of one dark eyebrow.

She smiled weakly. "They're just excited because exams are over and most of them will be going home tomorrow. You remember how it is, don't you?"

"Vaguely," was his amused answer. "Of course, at my *advanced* age . . ."

"I didn't mean that the way it sounded," she protested, laughing up at him. "I'm sure you're not so old you can't remember your college days."

"Not quite that old, but I am thirty-six. That's twelve years older than you. Do you think that's a great age difference?"

"No, I don't think it is," she said softly, puzzled by the slight nuance she had detected in his voice. His tone had lowered, subtly becoming more serious and intense. "Do you?"

"I'm sure I would have, until this afternoon," he replied as softly. "But meeting you has changed my thinking. Now I know just how intriguing a twenty-four year old woman can be."

Conversation was becoming too personal too swiftly again, and Laine was dismayed to find herself inexorably drawn to Nick. Seeking to lessen the appeal of his magnetic personality, she reminded herself that she would probably never see him again after this weekend, so her growing attraction to him should be wisely nipped in the bud right now. He was only a man she was guiding around campus. She wouldn't take his flirting seriously. Hoping to convey that impression, she gave him a bland smile, then preceded him out of the student center.

As they followed one of the winding cobbled paths that crossed the grassy commons, Laine slipped her hands into her pockets and breathed deeply of the fresh night air.

"Well, I've shown you just about everything Father particularly wanted you to see." Disturbed by Nick's lack of voiced response, she was compelled to ask, "What do you think so far? Has your uncle's money been well spent in your opinion?"

"It's not my opinion that matters really. It's the facts that I'll report to him that count," Nick evaded deftly. "You should understand, though, that Uncle Phil thinks of Latham exactly the way it was when he attended college here. In his mind, it hasn't changed, so I can't predict what he'll have to say about the student center, for instance. When he reminisces, he always emphasizes that discipline and serious study were the rule here. Recreation meant a quiet talk with friends at the tavern or a game of football or basketball. Since he hasn't visited the campus since the center was built, he might be surprised to learn that it houses Ping-Pong tables, electronic games, and a coffee shop with jukebox blaring."

The edge of Laine's teeth sank into her bottom lip as she gazed up at Nick's carved profile. Her hopes took a slight dip but she buoyed them up with her explanation. "Colleges have to be competitive to recruit students these days, especially small colleges like this. Recreational facilities are a necessity. Despite Latham's reputation for academic excellence, not many people would choose to come here if we only offered a football field and a basketball court. I'm sure you can see that?"

Nick's broad shoulders lifted in a slight shrug. "I might, but Uncle Phil is an avid traditionalist. He's happiest when institutions remain the same year after year."

"But times change. Being a successful businessman, he must realize that?"

Nick smiled indulgently. "He does, but to him Latham College has nothing to do with business. As I said before, he's amazingly sentimental about this place."

"But you're more objective," Laine persisted. "And since you're the person he trusted to come look us over, surely he'll be influenced by your opinion."

"Yes, I imagine he will be."

"And?"

"And what?"

"What kind of opinion will you give him?" Laine asked bluntly, slightly frustrated by his evasiveness. "Have you been at all impressed by what you've seen here so far?"

"No comment," Nick countered, laughing softly when she responded to his noncommittal answer with a disappointed sigh. To her amazement, he lifted one hand and ran it lightly over the silken hair that swept her forehead. Visible in the lamplit glow, his eyes glimmered with amusement. "Come, now, Laine, you can't expect me to form an opinion on the basis of this little tour. A million-dollar grant is nothing to be careless with. I'll need to talk to your father further and meet some of the faculty. And I'll want to see inside some of the buildings you've shown me tonight. You can see the logic in that, can't you?"

She could and she did but nodded in agreement somewhat reluctantly. It had been rather foolish of her to hope he would immediately decide Latham deserved his uncle's grant, but she had hoped he would nonetheless. Now she was forced to admit to herself what she had known intuitively all along: Nick Brannon didn't make hasty decisions. As he had told her himself, he was a very thorough man. Resigning herself to that vaguely worrisome truth, she unconsciously touched the hair he'd brushed his hand across and returned his knowing smile. "As I said, we've seen about all we can at night. Would you like to drop by the tavern now?"

"Show me where you work first," he requested with a grin. "I want to see where you have your clothes decorated with oatmeal cooky handprints."

Delighted by the prospect of guiding him through the building on campus she knew best, Laine launched into an enthusiastic testimonial to the nursery school. Her face was alight with animation as she told Nick how the school served the faculty and surrounding community by providing day care.

"And it's so helpful for the student assistants to get actual classroom experience," she continued, handing Nick her key to the four-room building as they ascended the steps. "Some of them have never dealt with small children before, but they learn how to here. Later, when they're assigned to some elementary school in the state to do their student teaching, they're always praised for their professionalism."

After Nick unlocked the door, Laine reached inside, flipped a switch, and walked into the lighted corridor. He followed, looking around with genuine interest.

"Are all your student assistants women?" he asked while she unlocked her own classroom. "Not many young men seem to want to teach primary age children, do they?"

"Unfortunately not. I wish more of them did want to, because I had a young man as an assistant last semester and he was terrific with the kids." Laine smiled reminiscently. "Looking at him, you would have imagined he'd rather play tackle on a pro football team. He was practically a giant, but the children adored him."

Nick chuckled wryly. "And I'm sure his sheer size helped maintain discipline."

"You could never hope to see more angelic children than they were when he was here. Made me wish I was big and brawny."

"What a waste that would be," Nick spoke quietly behind her, feathering his hands across her shoulders, lightly

41

exploring the finely sculptured structure. "No, I much prefer you the way you are, Laine."

With his touch, she had tensed. Now she hastily swung open her classroom door and stepped inside while turning on the lights. A resigned sigh escaped her when she saw the gaily colored pieces of a wooden puzzle scattered across the sturdy short-napped carpet near her desk. "Apparently my student assistants couldn't wait to start celebrating the end of term. They didn't even tidy up before they left," she tossed back over her shoulder as she hurried across the room. It was a weak excuse to put distance between herself and him and she knew it but decided it was better than no excuse at all. Sinking down onto her knees, she began gathering up the puzzle pieces and arranging them properly on their woodboard frame.

For a moment Nick remained in the doorway, hands in his pockets as he watched her. When she finished the puzzle and was laying it atop a low table, however, he came to her side, extending a helping hand as she started to stand.

Without hesitation, Laine placed her fingers against his palm and was drawn to her feet. She busily smoothed the skirt of her dress until Nick gently took her chin between thumb and forefinger, tilting her head back slightly. Her eyes met his. Suddenly she felt an attraction to him that was overwhelming in its intensity. Every fiber of her being seemed to have awakened with sensual awareness, and she knew he felt it too. Inexplicable excitement altered the rhythm of her heartbeat; it began to thud erratically. The building's silence surrounded them, creating an oddly intimate atmosphere. Trying to forget they were all alone, Laine forced herself to smile at him

"Do you know what I'd like to do?" she managed to ask, though somewhat breathlessly. Dragging her gaze from him, she looked at the doorway. "Down there, at the east end of the building, I'd love to be able to add another classroom, one for children with special needs. One's needed here. Special children in the surrounding communities have to be taken to Savannah to school. And our special education majors have no chance to really work with such children until they student-teach." She sighed. "To be honest, I'd practically convinced Father to use some of your uncle's grant this year to add a special-ed classroom."

"Laine, what a devious beguiling little witch you are," Nick murmured, smiling indulgently. "You're trying to shame me into advising my uncle to award that grant."

She had to return his smile while admitting, "Well, maybe I am. But I'm doing it for a good cause."

"Agreed. However . . ." He paused significantly, shaking his head at her rather crestfallen expression. "Laine, I'm not going to make a decision about the grant until I know a good deal more about Latham, no matter how many good causes you espouse."

"But we really need that classroom here, Nick," she argued earnestly. "This old building wasn't designed for the handicapped, but an addition would have its own outside entrance and restroom facilities for children in wheelchairs." As she continued to list the potential benefits of a special-education classroom, he listened patiently, but at last she saw she couldn't persuade him to award the grant. He had a million dollars to consider, and since the classroom wouldn't cost nearly that amount, her appeals for her pet project weren't really getting her anywhere. She fell silent and simply looked at him.

"Your classroom sounds like a fine idea," he said seriously. "I'll certainly keep it in mind."

Believing him, she nodded, knowing his serious consideration was the best she could hope for at the moment. "But I'll remind you about the classroom again," she promised, determination uptilting her chin. "In case you happen to forget."

"Zealot," he chided teasingly as they left the room together and Laine locked the door behind them.

Five minutes later, Laine and Nick crossed the square again and walked leisurely toward the old tavern across from the bookstore. Even before they reached the tavern they had frequent glimpses of the softly lighted interior when the heavy oak door swung open for new arrivals and the rare departure. A babble of excited voices, combined with muted background music, spilled out into the pristine silence of the square with every swing of the door. Inside, it was rather difficult to hear, so Laine practically had to shout when she asked Nick if he saw an empty table. His height was an advantage, and suddenly her small hand was clasped firmly into his much larger one and she was being pulled along with him as he threaded his way through the crowd. A tiny corner table had just been vacated.

"I'm afraid a waitress will never find us," Laine commented while she sat down in the chair Nick pulled out for her. "And if one sees us, she'll never get through that crowd."

Nick didn't hear. Draping one arm across the back of her chair, he bent down to listen as she repeated what she had just said. When he wisely informed her that he'd go to the bar and bring back their drinks, she nodded agreement. Watching him disappear in the sea of reveling students, Laine decided her father had made a mistake by suggesting they drop by here. Usually the tavern was a place for quiet relaxation, but the students were in no mood for quiet tonight. Freedom was at hand and they seemed to want to share their joy with anyone within a five-mile radius.

The combined aromas of pepperoni and mozzarella

filled the air, and Laine smiled to herself. She would probably never again smell pizza baking without thinking of this tavern. Waiting for Nick's return, she strummed her fingers lightly on the tabletop then smiled hello at one of her student assistants, Debby Wilson. The girl, much less shy than Mary Lou Baker, swooped down on Laine, her shoulder-length auburn hair bouncing.

"Who is that gorgeous man you came in with?" she nearly shouted in Laine's ear. "Is he new on the faculty or something? Will he be here next year?"

Laine shook her head. "Sorry to disappoint you, but he's just visiting campus briefly."

"Doesn't that just figure?" Debby yelled, pursing her mouth in an exaggerated pout. "All year long, I didn't have one good-looking instructor or professor." When Laine laughed aloud at the inadvertent insult, Debby's face went beet red. "Oh, but I didn't mean you, Miss Winthrop, really I didn't! You're a woman and you're very pretty. I was talking about the men."

Nodding, Laine smiled forgiveness then inclined her head toward Nick, who was threading his way back to her again. "Here comes gorgeous now."

"In that case . . ." Debby cast a longing glance at the tiny table. "I guess there's really only room enough for two here. Right? So I better move along before he gets here?"

Laine didn't insist Debby stay so the younger girl finally walked away after a rather dejected heaving of her shoulders.

Remembering Laine's preference, Nick brought her a glass of white wine along with a stein of beer for himself. Pulling his chair close to hers, he sat down, leaning his head to one side toward her. "This place reminds me of my long-lost youth."

"I didn't think you could remember back so far," she

quipped, raising the wine glass to her lips. "Senility and all . . ."

Further conversation consisted of a few words tossed in here and there. Coherent discussion was virtually impossible. After ten minutes or so, though over half Nick's beer remained in the stein, he took Laine's hand and stood, pulling her up with him. "Let's get out of here."

More than a little happy to leave, Laine breathed a relieved sigh a moment later when Nick swung open the oak door for her to precede him outside. After the fairly uncomfortable warmth of the tavern, the night air was chilling. Laine shivered and rubbed her bare arms briskly, then was promptly enfolded in Nick's jacket, which he had removed inside.

Murmuring her thanks, Laine wrapped the jacket more snugly about her to better appreciate the warmth and the pleasant mingling of subtle fragrances of lime aftershave and tobacco. "I'm sorry, but tonight wasn't a good time to come. Too much exuberance because the year's ending. It's usually not so noisy or crowded in there."

"I understand, thinking back about some of the college parties I attended. I just wasn't eager to relive them this evening. Hope you didn't mind leaving."

"Not at all," she assured him.

A long silence stretched between them, but it wasn't uncomfortable. Compared to the noisy tavern, the stillness of the star-studded night was welcome as they automatically walked back to Laine's house. Occasionally, she glanced out of the corner of her eye at Nick walking beside her. In the combined illumination of cresent moon and street lamp, his tan skin contrasted attractively with his white shirt where the strong column of his neck rose above his unbuttoned collar. Too soon, it seemed to Laine, they arrived at the foot of the walkway which led to the veranda. Nick stopped there.

Somewhat confused, Laine gazed up at him as she stopped too. "You're going in, aren't you? Or have you changed your mind about staying the night in the guest room?"

"I haven't changed my mind. It's too nice out here to go inside yet."

"Do you know the time? I left my watch on my dresser." When Nick told her it was nearly eleven, she was astounded. Time spent with Nick seemed to pass with incredible speed. "No wonder most of the lights in the house are out," she said softly. "Father's probably gone to bed already."

Nick said nothing. He moved closer to her and pointed heavenward to direct her attention to a falling star streaking across the black velvet sky.

"Umm. Lovely, isn't it?" she whispered.

"Very lovely," he whispered back.

Feminine instinct and the unusual huskiness of his voice made her overwhelmingly aware that he had been looking at her, not the sky, when he spoke. She looked at him, her eyes darting up to meet his, then lowering swiftly when she recognized the dangerous flicker of reflected moonlight in the dark green depths. He stepped closer, and she caught his right hand in both her own, knowing if she didn't, that hand would soon be on her and she might discover she very much liked being touched by him.

Tugging slightly at him, she started along the walkway. "It's late. We'd better go in now."

"Not yet, Laine," he said softly, pulling her back to him with incredible ease. Large but gentle hands slipped inside his jacket to span her trim waist and draw her against him.

The feel of his lean hard body was a truly physical assault on her senses. Her heart skipped several beats. Her breathing quickened as he molded her gently curved frame

47

to the firmer longer line of his. She tilted her head back to look up at him. "Nick, I . . ."

"Don't talk," he commanded, and when she started to anyway, he lowered his head to brush her lips with his.

Whatever words she managed to utter were captured, then totally forgotten. His kiss slowly, seductively, deepened in intensity until his hard mouth took complete possession of hers. Spreading warmth weakened her legs. When Nick gently nibbled the full tender curve of her lower lip, her soft moan of pleasure opened her mouth slightly to the persuasive power of his. Though she had been kissed before many times and occasionally liked it, never had any kiss affected her like this. Startled by her own intense desire to respond with total abandon, she tried to resist. She meant to push away from him, but instead her hands lingered on his shoulders. Fascinated by the contours of taut rippling muscles, she traced them tentatively, then cupped his neck in trembling hands. Her fingers tangled compulsively in the crisp clean hair brushing his nape and she pressed closer to him.

Nick's warm breath filled her throat as he half-groaned. Hard arms tightened around her slender supple form, and his kiss became as forceful as he himself sometimes was, plundering the soft sweetness of her lips with insistent, ever-increasing demand. One lean hand cradled the back of her head, allowing no escape from the compelling possession of his mouth. But she had no desire to escape— she felt too gloriously alive, all her senses aroused to total receptiveness. Nick's free hand was moving over her back, arching her to him, his fingertips exploring the delicate structure of bone and warm firm flesh and sending tremors of delight feathering up and down her spine. Every sensitized nerve ending conveyed his message of passion.

Yet Laine's passion didn't rise to equal his until his lips sought the curve of her slender neck. Before, his kiss, his

48

embrace had only been thrillingly electric, but when the tip of his tongue tasted the hollow at the base of her throat, he awakened primitive desire. Her breath caught when a shattering emptiness bloomed centrally within and clamored to be filled.

Resisting the dangerous lethargy that dragged at her, she turned her face into the warm hollow of his shoulder when he lifted his head, meaning to take possession of her mouth again. "No," she breathed and pushed lightly against his broad chest.

Nick's hands slipped slowly from her waist as he reluctantly released her. A faint smile of indulgence gentled his hard mouth.

Laine's answering smile was almost shy and her hand shook slightly as she gestured toward his car. "If you'll get your luggage, we can go in now and I'll show you to the guest room."

Silently, Nick complied and he didn't speak even as they entered the quiet house and Laine led him upstairs. While she flitted around the guest room to make certain all was in order, then showed him the door to the small adjoining bath, he stood and watched her, hands thrust into his pockets, his single suitcase on the floor by his feet.

Disconcerted by his watchful silence, Laine hastened to slip the jacket he had lent her off her shoulders. Willing herself to meet his intent gaze, she went to hand the coat to him, murmuring her thanks.

Warm eyes held hers captive as he inclined his head in a nod. Then he reached out one hand to slide his fingers into her flaxen tousled hair, an oddly caring gesture that did nothing to stabilize her heartbeat. Perhaps he knew that because he smiled faintly again as he nearly whispered, "Goodnight, Laine."

"Goodnight. I hope you'll be comfortable in here," she answered, managing to sound far more composed than she felt. Her gait deliberately unhurried, she went out, pulling his door shut behind her. Then she rushed across the hall to her own room, where she was finally able to take several deep, self-controlling breaths. Catching sight of her reflection in her vanity mirror, she wrinkled her nose impatiently. So, all right, Nick Brannon *was* a fascinating man. She was impressed by his dedication to a noble career and she was unquestionably drawn to him by the sheer force of his magnetic personality. Despite all that, she shouldn't be in such a dither about a kiss, even if it had been the most pleasurable she'd ever experienced. After all, during the time Nick had held her close to him his hands hadn't once wandered indiscriminately, but now it disturbed her to think of how she might have responded if they had. She surely would have resisted, she tried to tell herself as she went to take a bath.

Thirty minutes later, soothed to sleepiness by a leisurely soak in warm salt-scented water, Laine put on the ivory silk chemise Regina had sent her for Christmas. Its hem brushed the tops of her thighs, and though it was an unnecessarily sexy garment for one who slept alone, she couldn't resist wearing it. The fabric was so luxuriously soft against her skin. Stifling a yawn, Laine went to the vanity to quickly brush her hair, then walked over to her bed. Before she could draw back the sheet, however, the sudden shrill ringing of the phone in the hallway downstairs halted her progress. Sure it must be a wrong number at this late hour, she rushed from her room to answer before the ringing awakened her father.

Only Nick's quick reflexes saved them from a collision. His hands quickly spanned her waist, halting her midstride.

"It may be for me," he said very quietly. "I left this number with my service."

Before Laine could answer, the ringing ceased and her

father's voice drifted up from the hallway. Nick murmured an apology for the late-night call but she didn't have the presence of mind to acknowledge it, because as he spoke his darkening gaze moved slowly over her. She realized then that she was clad in practically nothing and he was shirtless. Automatically, her hands had come up to press against his chest when he'd stopped her from running into him and now the heat of his bronze hair-roughened skin seemed to sear her palms. She bit back a gasp as strong fingers began to massage the appealing arch between her waist and gentle outcurving of her hips.

"Damn," he muttered roughly, eyes glinting. "I doubt I'll get much sleep tonight, knowing you're just across the hall wearing no more than that."

Thornton Winthrop interrupted the intimacy of the moment. "A call for you, Nick," he said as he came up the stairs. He stopped short and stared when he saw his daughter nearly in the arms of the man in the hallway.

When Nick released her, Laine turned and stepped back into her room, without ever having said a word to either man. Leaning back against her door, she pressed her hands against exceedingly hot cheeks. Though her heartbeat was getting back to normal, she no longer felt the least bit sleepy. Nick Brannon was very adept at disturbing her equilibrium, and Laine smiled to herself. She was beginning to look forward to going to the party with him tomorrow evening.

Humming softly, she started across the room toward her bed but stopped and spun around when someone tapped on her door then began opening it. It was only her father who entered, however, so she was able to breathe again.

Tightening the belt of his bathrobe, Thornton eyed her speculatively, either not noticing the faint revealing blush that tinged her cheeks or ignoring it. He raked his fingers through his silvery hair. "Well, how did it go tonight?" he asked finally. "Did Nick seemed impressed with the campus? Is he going to give us the grant?"

"He says he wants to see more before he makes that decision, Father. As to whether or not he was impressed tonight, I really couldn't tell."

"Well, I can tell he's certainly impressed by you," he said meaningfully. "I'm sure that'll help."

"I wouldn't count on that," Laine replied with an uncharacteristic sharpness.

Thornton irritably shook his head. "You know very little about men, Laine, if you believe that. Women can influence them in everything. Your mother could have persuaded me to do anything. And I have no doubt you can influence Nick Brannon. He's so obviously interested in you. All you have to do is encourage him."

Unease stole over Laine as she wondered just what her father meant. Exactly how far would he want her to go in encouraging Nick? Afraid to ask him, totally uncertain now what his answer might be, she merely shrugged her shoulders. "I still think you're wrong, Father. I won't be able to influence Nick, though I'll certainly be friendly and cordial to him during his stay."

"Cordial isn't good enough," Thornton said bluntly on his way out of her room. "This grant's vital to Latham, so you'd better be as nice to Brannon as you can."

As the door was pulled firmly shut, Laine ran a hand over her hair and sighed dejectedly. Somehow, her father had tainted the magic of the evening. Her anticipation of tomorrow night with Nick had somewhat dimmed. Her father was beginning to make her feel as if she were no more than a pawn in the high-stakes game two men were playing.

By seven-thirty Saturday night, Laine was ready for the

faculty party. After once again ordering her to be very nice to Nick, Thornton went ahead, leaving the two of them alone in the house together. In her room Laine procrastinated, rebrushing her hair to delay at least for a few minutes the time when she would have to go downstairs where Nick awaited her. She had hardly seen him all day. While her father had taken him on a more extensive tour of the campus, she had given the house a lick and a promise and then begun the student assistant evaluations. Unfortunately she still had more than half of them to complete. Normally she would have skipped tonight's party to work, but she couldn't do that now. Nick was waiting.

Her mother's white crocheted shawl over her arm, Laine went down. Seeing Nick's suitcase sitting beside the front door, she frowned as she walked into the living room to find him. "Why the suitcase?" she asked as he immediately arose from his chair. "Are you going back to Savannah after the party?"

"No, I'm checking into the motel," he explained, flipping back the sides of his navy blazer to slip his hands into the pockets of gray trousers. "I don't want any more late-night calls disturbing you and your father."

"Oh, but Father must've been awake anyhow," Laine assured him. "Or he wouldn't have answered the phone so fast. I'm sure he didn't mind. In fact, I'm sure he'd insist that you stay here for the rest of your visit."

Though Nick thanked her for the proffered hospitality, he declined. "A motel room is best," he said firmly, while inspecting her white cotton dress with ruffled tier skirt and tiny stand-up lace collar that encircled her long slender neck. Never taking his eyes from her, he came across the room. "You're lovely, Laine," he said very softly, then gave her a disturbingly secretive smile. "Innocent-looking yet provocative too, a very tantalizing combination."

53

Gasping as he reached out to trace one fingertip along the outer edges of the see-through lace yoke that extended down nearly to the beginning swell of her breasts, she took a jerky step backward, away from him. "We'd better go," she suggested, her voice a breathy whisper. "We wouldn't want to be late."

Still smiling, Nick acquiesced, indicating with a gesture that she should precede him to the door, taking his suitcase with him as they went out. After stowing it in the trunk of his car, he lightly clasped Laine's left hand when they started toward the tavern, rented by the faculty for the evening.

Still slightly uncomfortable about what had happened between them in the hallway last night, Laine said nothing for several moments, but at last she could contain her curiosity no longer. "Well, how'd the tour go today?" she asked eagerly. "Do you think Latham deserves your uncle's grant this year?"

"As I advise juries—make no decisions until all evidence is in," he answered calmly, telling her absolutely nothing in the process. Then he adroitly changed the subject. "How was your day? Ready to post grades Monday?"

"I wish," she replied with a rather tired sigh. "I didn't even finish half the evaluations today."

Nick gazed down at her, his expression inscrutable. "You obviously take your work very seriously. Do you demand as much from your assistants as you do from yourself? Any unfavorable evaluations today?"

Laine shook her head. "That's a good thing about being in the education department. The career prospects for teachers are limited these days, so most of our students are quite dedicated. I can usually find some ability in all of them to at least give them an average evaluation."

"Fair-minded Laine," he murmured, only half teasingly. "And do you always look for the best in people?"

54

"I try," her tone was a bit more defensive than she had intended. She wondered what he was driving at.

"You're not very close to your father, are you?" Nick asked too perceptively. His gaze was steady, unreadable, as her azure eyes darted up to meet his. "Is he closer to your sister Regina?"

Laine smiled rather wistfully. "I don't really think Father's ever been close to anyone except my mother. But he does sort of idolize Regina."

The firm line of Nick's jaw hardened. "And would you do anything to try to please him?"

"Heavens, no!" Laine's accompanying laugh sounded a bit bleak. "Just ask him. He thinks I've always been the most frustrating child."

"But you'd like to please him?" Nick persisted gently.

Luckily, Laine could use their arrival at the tavern as an excuse not to answer. Pretending his question was driven out of her mind, she gave him a mischievous smile. "Let me warn you, you'll probably be mobbed by all the women here tonight. The whole campus has been abuzz since you came yesterday. It isn't every day that a nationally known attorney visits Latham."

"Laine, we *are* going to discuss your relationship with your father," Nick began tautly, but before he finished, she scooted ahead of him and into the tavern.

Her warning proved correct. The moment their arrival at the party was noticed, Dean Jacobs's wife, Dulcie, swooped down on Nick with an excessively enthusiastic welcome. Tucking one chubby hand around his arm, she promptly dragged him toward her chattering group of friends and away from Laine.

For the next two and a half hours, Laine only caught glimpses of Nick. Dulcie Jacobs was acting as if he had escorted her to the party and was introducing him around as if he were a close personal friend. It was by far the most boring party Laine had ever attended. Everytime she turned around she had to hear about Nick.

Marge Simmons voiced Laine's unspoken observation. As they sat alone together sometime after ten, the older woman watched Dulcie and her friends encircle Nick and heaved a sigh of dismay. "Really, I don't think the faculty can be making a very good impression on Mr. Brannon. I wish they'd stop fawning over him."

"So do I, but I guess their behavior's understandable," Laine responded with a resigned shrug. "After all, everyone here wants Latham to receive that grant. And besides, they've probably read about him in the newspapers. He's something of a celebrity."

"And they're acting like starstruck adolescents. Quite frankly, I'm embarrassed," Marge said, then shrugged herself. "Well, I can't do anything about their actions, can I? So tell me, is Mr. Brannon nice? Do *you* think he'll give us the grant?"

"I really don't know," Laine admitted, then tensed as she gazed past Marge. One hand fluttered nervously on the tabletop. "All I know is that's he's headed this way and he certainly doesn't look all that pleased."

"Oh, dear. See you later then," Marge whispered then abandoned her friend before Nick even reached his destination.

A second later Laine was sitting quite still, transfixed by hard green eyes and a tan carved face, devoid of expression. When Nick reached for her hand, she extended her left automatically and stood as strong fingers pressed impellingly against her palm.

"We've stayed long enough to satisfy convention," he announced tersely. "We're leaving now."

Dulcie Jacobs made their exit no easy accomplishment. At least she tried, but Nick blocked her interference with a pleasantly spoken lie. "Laine and I have other plans for the rest of the evening. Thank you for having me here tonight. You've been a most attentive hostess, Mrs. Jacobs."

"Too attentive maybe?" Laine suggested while being gently impelled out of the tavern.

"Mrs. Jacobs nearly talked my ear off," Nick replied, sounding somewhat exasperated. "I applaud her involvement in the arts, but I didn't need to hear about every art council and theater committee she's served on since the beginning of time."

Laine fought a grin. "You should feel honored. Dulcie only tries to impress people she considers very important. She rarely bothers to speak to peasants like me."

"No doubt. That's one reason she's incredibly boring. I prefer people who don't put on airs."

"I know how irritating she can be," Laine commiserated as they approached the Winthrop house. "And I'm sorry you didn't enjoy the party."

"The evening can still be salvaged." A rather disconcerting secretive smile played over Nick's lips as he looked down at Laine, catching her hand in his. "We'll drive to the coast. A friend of mine has a house along the waterway. From the beach you can see Sapelo Island, and he won't mind if we go enjoy the view."

"That sounds wonderful," Laine murmured, and it did. Though she had to wonder if it wasn't insanity to agree to visit a secluded moonlit beach with Nick, she couldn't muster the will power to refuse his invitation. And when he took acquiescence for granted by opening the passenger door of his silver Jaguar sedan for her, she slipped into the seat without hesitation, much less protest.

Several minutes later a glimmering ribbon of black highway stretched out before their headlights as they traveled northeast. Nick drove as he did everything else: smoothly, competently, and with a relaxed self-confidence

57

that allowed him to guide the powerful Jaguar with only one lean hand draped over the steering wheel. More than once Laine caught herself gazing at that hand and the other, remembering how she had felt last night when Nick had kissed her and those same hands had evoked her surprisingly ardent response. The mere memory quickened her pulse rate. With concentrated effort she turned to look out the window into the mysterious dark depths of the pine forest that bordered the roadway.

Flowing through the open windows, the cool night air stirred Laine's freshly washed hair, and the muted swish of the tires plus soft music from the car stereo began to quiet her lingering doubts about coming on this drive with Nick. Resting back in the leather seat, she turned her head to smile at him.

"Umm. It's a lovely night, isn't it? Cool enough to have the windows open, instead of turning on the air conditioner." She took a long deep breath, then exhaled slowly. "Fresh air's so much nicer, don't you think?"

For an instant, Nick glanced at her, his features etched in the dim dash light. Though he turned his attention back to the road again almost immediately, he reached for her left hand then brought it over to rest in his on a muscular thigh.

His silent answering nod and his thumb, playing idly over Laine's fingertips, reawakened all her misgivings. Relaxing was next to impossible now, and as she unconsciously stared at Nick's profile, she understood once again why she sometimes felt so uneasy with him. There was a potential for ruthlessness in him, evidenced by that chiseled face and by the straightforward, unapologetic glint that shone in his eye. A man of indomitable will, he might prefer to employ finesse in accomplishing his goals, but Laine knew instinctively that he would be perfectly capable of taking what he wanted should the need arise.

This realization was disconcerting, yet she didn't even attempt to insist he take her home. Intrinsically honest as she was with herself, she knew she really wanted to be with him tonight, despite the slight trepidation she now felt, despite the potential consequences. Conflicting emotions, apprehension and anticipation, battled within her as they passed through a small coastal village where weathered houses dreamed beneath a starry sky and fishing boats bobbed gently in the marina. But it was the apprehension that was diminished and the anticipation that was heightened when Nick turned off the highway just beyond the village onto a white pebbled private drive. Live oaks, festooned with Spanish moss, met overhead, enclosing them in a tunnel as Nick drove on more slowly. A feeling of total isolation began to grip Laine, and when they rounded a curve in the drive and she saw the dark, obviously unoccupied bungalow sprawled out before them, she tensed.

Her reaction was duly noticed and read correctly. "You're right. No one's here," Nick said calmly, releasing her hand. "This is a summer house and Bill doesn't usually move his family in until mid-June."

"Oh. I see. A summer house must be nice. Do you own one too?"

The Jaguar glided to a smooth stop and Nick turned off the engine as he nodded. "You could call it a summer house but I'd prefer to live there all the time. Though my offices are in Atlanta and I own a house there, I think of my place on St. Simons Island as home."

"St. Simons. Isn't that a coincidence? Our family used to vacation there sometimes. Well, we did until . . . my mother died. After that, Father took Regina and me back only once. I guess there were just too many memories there."

With a compassionate nod, Nick got out of the car then came around to help her out. Leaving her a moment, he went to take a plaid throw from the the trunk. When he returned, he casually placed a hand against the small of her back to direct her along the flagstone that wound around to the front of the elegant shingled bungalow. About thirty feet beyond they stepped into sand, and Laine nearly stumbled when her heels sank. Laughing, she held onto Nick's arm as she slipped out of first one shoe then the other, then padded barefoot across the beach with him. As he spread the blanket, she dug one foot into the cool sand and lifted it, allowing the fine grains to trickle between her toes.

For several moments Nick watched her before reaching up to take her hands and draw her down beside him. A salt scented breeze caressed them. The pale light of the cresent moon shimmered on the waters of the intracoastal waterway. To the south, in the distance, Sapelo Island was silhouetted against the night sky, its ancient live oaks standing sentinel over a band of salt marshes.

Settling herself more comfortably, Laine leaned back on her hands and extended her shapely, lightly tanned legs out before her, watching as Nick plucked a sea oat from the sand and twirled it thoughtfully. When he obviously became aware of her intent observation, he turned his head to meet her bemused gaze.

"You wouldn't let a snob like Dulcie Jacobs influence your decision about the grant, would you?" Laine blurted out, feeling the sudden need to make any kind of conversation. "I mean, she . . ."

"That woman's personality will have nothing to do with my decision," Nick interjected firmly. "But speaking of the grant, I think you should know I plan to call in an auditor before I decide anything."

Laine sat up straight. "You can't possibly suspect my father has been misusing the money your uncle donates!"

"You're jumping to conclusions. I don't suspect your

father or anyone else of anything. An audit's simply a wise precaution."

"Sometimes I wonder if you really want to award the grant to Latham," Laine said pointedly. "If you're your uncle's heir, I guess a million-dollar grant is just a million dollars less you'll receive from his estate someday."

Moving with lithe swiftness, Nick turned and grasped the back of her head in one strong hand, forcing her to look up and thus recognize the dark thunderous expression on his face. "And to think I called you fair-minded," he nearly growled. "I think you should know that if you repeated that ridiculous statement in front of witnesses, I could sue you for slander and win, because I'm *not* heir to my uncle's estate. My cousin Sara, Uncle Phil's daughter, will inherit everything. I didn't come to Latham to guard my own self-interests."

Laine's entire body burned with embarrassment. She felt a perfect fool. "That was a despicable thing to say and I'm sorry," she whispered contritely. "It was just an idea that popped into my mind and out of my mouth before I really thought about it. I guess it's because this grant's so important for Latham. Maybe you can't really understand that, since you've always had money."

"Wrong again," he cut in bitingly. "My uncle has money. My parents aren't wealthy, never have been. I worked my way through law school."

Laine groaned softly, feeling twice the fool now. The tip of her tongue touched her lips as she gazed up into his piercing eyes. "I guess I have been jumping to conclusions, haven't I?" she murmured. "I'm truly sorry."

Nick's grip loosened slightly as he said, "Believe it or not, I can remember the time when a million dollars seemed like much more money than it does to me now."

"Then perhaps you can forgive me for sounding so awful."

Nick relented. His fingers in her hair became caressing, slipping through the silken strands that framed the appealingly small face upturned to his. "Right now," he said roughly, "I could probably forgive you anything."

Her heart leaped against her breastbone as the angry light in his eyes flared to fiery passion. "Why?" she breathed.

"Because you're so . . ." He didn't finish. When her hands came up to cup his neck, he slowly pulled her to him. With the gentle yet demanding pressure of the edge of his thumb against her chin, he tugged her mouth open slightly to receive his kiss. Deliberately teasing, he brushed firm lips slowly back and forth across hers until her breathing quickened and her arms slipped up around his neck.

With a muffled murmur of triumph he bore her down onto the blanket, his mouth devouring the soft shape of hers, his tongue tasting the sweetness within. As he probed the tender veined flesh of her inner lower lip, a thrill of delight shot through Laine, so intense that her legs went weak. The evocative weight of Nick's torso pressed her down. The sand beneath the blanket yielded, as did her softness to the hard masculine line of his chest. Still cradling her head in one hand, he moved the other upward over her, following the swell of her hips into the narrow insweeping waist and onward to the rapid rise and fall of firm cushioned breasts. His palm brushed lightly as a feather over one then the other, bringing her body to life with exquisite sensations. With Laine's soft gasp of pleasure, he traced a fingertip around the hardening peaks outlined against the fabric of her dress.

Laine strained against him, unable to get near enough as he kissed her again and again, long searching passionate kisses that seemed to demand total surrender. Firm taking lips gently twisted the tender shape of hers; strong even

62

teeth nibbled their softness until even the complete possession of his mouth was no longer enough for him . . . or for her. She clung to him when he moved over onto his side, turning her with him. And she offered no murmur of protest as he slowly lowered the back zipper of her dress. The night air cooled her overheated skin when Nick pushed the dress from her shoulders, off her arms, and down to drape around her waist. Laine shivered as the top of her slip met the same fate, but when Nick arched her to him and his lips explored the fragile contours of her shoulders, scattering hot kisses into the enticing hollows, her entire body was suffused with warmth again. Her arms went eagerly around his waist, her hands wandering over him, massaging and caressing his broad back. His heated flesh seemed to sear her fingertips, kindling a central consuming fire inside her. She discovered she liked to touch as much as she liked being touched by him.

Even when her bra was unhooked and the lace cups were slowly peeled away, Laine didn't resist. Yet she caught her breath, overwhelmed with a sense of utter vulnerability as one of Nick's hands curved over her right hipbone, pressing down onto her back again. Her eyes fluttered open, luminously shy while Nick swept a hungry gaze over her. He stroked the perfect curves of her breasts with his fingertips, then traced the roseate peaks and teased the hard nubs with his thumbs. His narrowed gaze captured and held hers.

She didn't breathe again until he smiled down at her. Then a joyous wonder enveloped her and she lifted her arms invitingly to him, whispering, "Kiss me again, Nick."

He did. His mouth descended on hers with ravishing force. When she began to give him back kiss for kiss then tried to unbutton his shirt, he gently pushed aside her trembling hand to undo the buttons himself much more

63

quickly. Laine's nails caught in the fine dark hair on his chest as her fingers tentatively explored the taut muscles. With a muffled groan, Nick released her lips, slipped an arm beneath her back, and arched her breasts upward.

When he lowered his head, Laine breathed an urgent "No."

"Yes, Laine, I have to," he muttered relentlessly. His mouth enclosed the rose-colored tumescent peak of one breast then the other, again and again, until both were throbbing with exquisite sensation and she was warm and weak and all yielding femininity. Entangling her fingers in his hair, she urged his mouth up to hers again, and she only fully realized exactly what she was inviting when she felt the weight of one of his legs entangling with her own, and she felt his passion surge against her.

As she trembled violently, Nick tensed, then pushed himself up, away from her. "This has to stop now or it won't stop at all."

Laine was unwilling to let him go completely. One hand feathered down his back when he sat up beside her as she whispered entreatingly, "Couldn't you just kiss me once more?"

"For God's sake, surely you know I need a lot more than a kiss from you now," he muttered with some impatience. His expression was grim as he looked down at her. "But it's too soon for you to give me what I want."

She stroked his arm. "But Nick . . ."

"You're not ready for that, Laine," he interrupted tersely. "Even if your father did order you to be nice to me."

With her swift intake of breath, the color drained from Laine's face with frightening speed. She stiffened as humiliation killed all desire and she jerkily folded her arms across her bare breasts. For a long moment she stared mutely up at Nick, and when she finally managed to speak, her voice was choked. "You heard what Father said to me tonight. You heard him!"

"Yes." Nick's piercing eyes bored into hers. "I'd started up the stairs and he was standing just outside your room."

"But you can't think that I . . . that all this tonight was because . . ." Her words broke off as he turned his head. For an instant, anger replaced humiliation. He had no right to assume she had responded to him for her father's benefit! Indignant, she sat up, clutching her dress up around her. "You'd better take me home now," she said in a tight, cool voice.

"Good idea. Get dressed," he commanded, buttoning his shirt as he rose to his feet.

A few minutes later, by the time they were driving toward campus, Laine was more hurt than angry. Relaxing back in the leather passenger seat, she felt sapped of all strength. Why had this had to happen *after* she'd discovered she was so attracted to Nick because she truly liked and respected him? Glancing out of the corner of her eye, she winced when she recognized the intractable set of Nick's strong jaw as he stared straight ahead. Though she longed to make him believe he was totally wrong about what had happened tonight, she had no idea how to begin explaining the truth to him. What could she say to a man who actually thought she was capable of prostituting herself because her father was determined to receive a million-dollar grant?

CHAPTER FOUR

It was a busy Monday morning. After Laine posted student assistant grades outside the door of her classroom, she began the last official task of the semester—completing data forms for the central computer that stored student records and issued those dreaded semester reports, predominated by all-important grade point averages. The transference of names, student identification numbers, and grades from Laine's records to the proper forms was tedious and required very little real concentration. Laine's mind started to wander, unfortunately to thoughts of Nick.

The humiliation she had suffered Saturday night still lingered, and she felt a growing resentment toward her father for placing her in such an awkward position. Treating her as if she were a child, he had felt the need to constantly remind her to be nice to Nick and that last indiscreet reminder Saturday night, which had been overheard, had undoubtedly cast both father and daughter in a bad light. Now Nick had reason to doubt that Laine's response to him had been genuine. His respect for her father had to have been diminished. It was even possible that Thornton had lessened Latham's chances of receiving the grant; if so, he had indeed made an unfortunate gaffe. The college would certainly suffer from the loss of a million dollars.

In actuality, however, Latham's financial health wasn't foremost in Laine's mind. She found herself far more concerned about Nick's opinion of her personally. What he thought of her had suddenly become of great importance and she was dismayed by the strange sense of vulnerability that had overtaken her since Saturday night. All her life she had ignored her own father's vague disapproval of her, but Nick's wasn't so easily dismissed. Perhaps because she felt the utmost respect for him, she needed to know he respected her too. It was fairly obvious that he didn't, though, she thought bleakly, recalling the hard chill she had detected in his deep voice when he'd said good-bye Saturday night. Staring blindly out her window, she slowly twirled her pen between thumb and forefinger, and a fleeting expression of anguish passed over her face. Exhaling a heartfelt sigh that stirred the wisps of hair that swept to the side across her brow, she shook her head, as if to dismiss all disturbing thought, and began to double-check the grades she had transferred from her records to the data forms.

Five minutes later the forms were securely tucked into a manila envelope, ready to be taken to the administration building. Fortunately, before Laine's thoughts could once again turn to Nick, Marge appeared in the office doorway, her face flushed, her expression harried.

"Are you finished?" she asked, her eyes brightening when Laine nodded. "Thank goodness. You can help in the nursery then. Polly Deacon started sneezing like crazy, and since we certainly don't want a summer cold epidemic around here, I sent her home. And if Dora doesn't get some help in the nursery, she swears she'll quit."

Laine laughed. "Can't say I'd blame her. I do need to take these forms to Chandler Hall before I step in though."

· "I'll send my secretary over with them. You go to Dora," Marge insisted. "I just left her, her patience wearing very thin."

With a nod and a wry understanding smile, Laine followed Maggie from the office then went swiftly to Nursery II. Even outside in the hallway the ruckus inside the room was clearly audible, proving that the children were taking advantage of the situation: Dora was alone and couldn't really watch all of them. When Laine opened the door and stepped inside, however, even the rowdiest of the children immediately lowered their voices an octave or two.

For the next hour or so a semblance of peace reigned in the room. Though it was never completely quiet, since the confined space held twelve toddlers, aged two to four years, whose collective energy knew no bounds. As Laine watched her six charges fidget ceaselessly while she read them a story, she could only be glad that the infants and very young toddlers were down the hall in Nursery I.

At ten o'clock Dora reluctantly informed Laine that it was time for outdoor activities, and together they led the children down the hall and out into the fresh air of the playground. Dora organized a game of London Bridge for the older toddlers while Laine presented an assortment of push-and-pull toys to the four children younger than two and a half. Naturally enough, two of the three boys wanted to play with the one plastic lawn mower. A furious tug-of-war ensued. Bradley yanked the mower toward him, then shrieked with ear-splitting shrillness when his rival, Charles, retaliated by biting his arm. Laine intervened, separating the two children as she sternly reprimanded Charles for biting. When she wouldn't allow either Brad or Charles to have the toy mower, Charles promptly flew into a tantrum, stamping his feet as he flailed his arms He accidentally struck Susie, who was innocently pulling a wagonload of plastic blocks past him.

When Susie lost her balance, sat down hard, and began to howl, Charles's tantrum abruptly terminated. His big brown eyes met the ice blue of Laine's.

"Sit down right there on the grass and be still," Laine commanded, and Charles obeyed as she swept Susie up in her arms. The little girl wrapped arms and legs around Laine and buried her wet face in her neck. Murmuring comforting words, Laine stroked the child's back until her sobs began to subside, becoming soft hiccoughing sounds. Even then, Susie clung tightly, pressing her small warm body hard against Laine, especially when Charles tried to make amends by getting up and coming to clutch a fistful of Laine's skirt and gaze hopefully up at her.

She had to smile forgiveness. And after reaching down to rumple his hair, she glanced up toward the rear door of the building, her heart doing a crazy little somersault when she saw Nick coming across the playground.

How untidy she must look, she thought, aware that her hair must be tousled and knowing the gentle wind was molding the thin cotton of her skirt against her slim shapely thighs, outlining them. Yet there was nothing to be done to improve her appearance at the moment. Wishing she could feel as composed as she was trying to appear, she watched expectantly while Nick strode toward her, soon diminishing the distance between them.

Nick stopped directly before Laine, close enough to reach out and touch her—but he didn't. He didn't smile either. He simply swept a disruptive gaze slowly over her until at last his eyes met hers.

Sheer nervous anticipation prompted Laine to smile at him. "Hi. I didn't expect to see you here," she said as matter-of-factly as possible. "Actually, I thought you were leaving Latham early this morning."

Nick shook his head. "The trial in Savannah doesn't reconvene until tomorrow, but I'll probably start back before lunch anyway. I wanted to talk to you first, though, if you're not too busy."

"No, not really," Laine responded, disentangling Charles's fingers from her skirt to clasp his chubby hand. "I'll just take the kids to Dora. Be right back."

A moment later, Laine returned to Nick. Inclining his head toward an oak tree in the corner of the playground, he placed one hand lightly against the small of her back as they walked toward the shade.

"That midday sun is hot, isn't it?" Laine said conversationally, using the opportunity to quickly smooth her flaxen hair. "Ah, but it's much cooler here in the shade."

Leaning one shoulder against the tree's rough bark, hands in his pockets, Nick looked down into her wide azure eyes, his gaze never wavering, as if he were seeking an answer to some unasked question in their depths. His will was unmistakably strong and growing stronger every second he prolonged the disturbing eye contact. At last he became the victor in the curiously unspoken battle and as Laine averted her gaze to stare instead at the V of smooth bronze skin exposed by his open collar, he spoke at last.

"I suppose the nursery school's kept open year round?" he asked casually, and when Laine nodded, he continued: "But surely you won't be as busy during the summer sessions as you are during the regular school year?"

Looking up at his lean tanned face again, Laine shook her head and smiled. "Fortunately, summers are pretty quiet. I'll have one four-year kindergarten class, but only half days, so I'll only have two student assistants. That makes evaluations at the end of the session easy enough. What about you? How's your summer shaping up?"

"Not too busy this year for once. I planned it that way. I expect this trial in Savannah to end sometime next week, and after that I should have over three weeks free and clear. Barring emergencies, of course."

"Frequent emergency calls are the price you have to pay for being a famous attorney, I guess," Laine said softly, wondering where this particular conversation was leading. Intuition told her it was leading somewhere, told her that Nick had something more he wanted to say, but an extended silence followed her last remark. Nick was looking out over the top of her head, toward center campus, his expression thoughtful and mysterious. Able to observe him freely, Laine examined the strong clean-cut features of his face and the long masculine line of his body. Virile, superbly fit, he was a man women would always stare at, and Laine found that she was hardly an exception. He was so damnably attractive. Remembering Saturday night, she longed to touch him, to feel his arms go swiftly around her again, but when he finally looked down at her—apparently sensing her intense appraisal—she hastily pushed her fantasies to the back of her mind.

"I should be going now," he announced abruptly, withdrawing his hands from his pockets as he stood up straight. "I only wanted to stop by here before I left to thank you for your hospitality this weekend."

So polite, Laine thought bleakly, as polite as one would be to a stranger. But she didn't feel like a stranger to him—Saturday evening wasn't an evening she would easily forget. To him, though, what had happened between them apparently meant little or nothing. Despite her extreme disappointment in the impersonal courtesy he was displaying, she concealed her reaction and gave him a polite smile.

Nick stepped away from her. "As I told your father this morning, the decision about the grant may take several weeks," he said quietly. "Thanks again for your hospitality. Good-bye, Laine."

Suddenly, Laine couldn't allow him to leave her in such a cool, unfeeling way. Although she had only known Nick

71

Brannon for a weekend, that weekend somehow seemed a lifetime. He had touched something deep inside her, aroused emotions and sensations she had never before experienced; in that moment, she admitted to herself that her feelings for him were deep and intense and overpowering. Reaching out, she laid her hand on his forearm, sensual excitement coursing hotly through her veins as muscles went taut beneath her fingers. She met his questioning gaze directly while allowing herself the luxury of looking deeply into his discerning emerald eyes. When a strange light flared within them and Nick caught her small hand in both of his, she automatically moved a step toward him.

"I guess it doesn't really matter to you," she murmured softly, sparkles dancing over her skin as the ball of one thumb moved slowly over the back of her hand. "But it matters to me what you think of me. And so . . . well, what I mean is, Saturday night didn't happen because I was trying to please Father. It was only you I was thinking about. My father never crossed my mind."

"Perhaps not consciously, but I wonder just how badly you subconsciously want to please him," Nick responded solemnly. "That's something I think you must seriously ask yourself." He released her hand, only to cup her chin, tilting her face upward as he lowered his head. His lips caressed hers more with tenderness than passion. Then he released her and turned to walk away. "Good-bye, Laine. I'll be in touch soon."

Laine watched him go, an unhappiness more painful than it should have been becoming a constricting ache in her chest. She leaned back against the tree trunk and took a deep tremulous breath. Nick would not be in touch soon, she knew it. Not for a moment did she believe she would ever hear from him again. That kiss had felt too much like a final good-bye.

* * *

Wednesday afternoon, nine days later, Laine hurried home from the nursery school, trying to beat the coming rain. Thunder rumbled overhead, becoming increasingly louder and more ominous as the sky thickened with inky dark clouds. The weather rather matched Laine's mood. For the past few days she had felt irritated with herself for not being able to simply forget all about Nick Brannon. Although she was managing to think of him less often, sometimes his unbidden image would appear in her mind's eye, preoccupying her once again with thoughts of him. It really was silly. How could she have become so enamored with a man she had only known two days? Laine didn't understand it; she was the practical, sensible Winthrop daughter. It was Regina who became infatuated with men at the drop of a hat. But Regina also lost interest in them as quickly. Laine wasn't having as much luck losing interest in Nick. And she was chiding herself mentally about that as she walked home.

"Oh, blast," she muttered as fat raindrops began to plop down just as she reached the lane to her house. She shot homeward in a sprint, her straw shoulder purse bouncing against her left hipbone with every stride. With luck, she outraced the deluge and stood for several minutes on the porch watching gray sheets of rain pound the trees, grass, and street. Then, inhaling the pungent scent of rich earth the rain had stirred up, she went into the house to change clothes and begin preparing dinner.

Laine was in the kitchen when Thornton arrived home an hour later. She could hear him muttering to himself while he thrust his umbrella forcefully into the stand in the foyer. Wondering what had aggravated him now, she walked down the hall toward him, delicately arched brows lifted questioningly.

"Hello, Father. Something wrong?"

"Damned umbrella," he muttered crossly. "The catch

73

is broken. Blasted thing keeps collapsing around my head."

"I'll buy you a new one when I'm in Brunswick Saturday," Laine said, fighting a smile. "If it rains again before then and the umbrella collapses, just try to pretend it's one of those pointed straw Oriental hats."

Thornton wasn't particularly amused by her suggestion. Silence was his response as he left her to go into the living room to get himself a drink. Laine followed, watching as he graciously poured her a small glass of white wine.

When Thornton brought the wine to her, he complained, "Brannon's certainly taking his sweet time making a decision about the grant. Heard nothing today."

"But he did tell you it would be several weeks, didn't he, Father?"

Thornton conceded that point with a nod, then eyed Laine speculatively. "However, I thought perhaps you would hear from him personally. Not about the grant, but if you did hear from him, you might be able to tell whether or not he's leaning toward awarding it. He hasn't been in touch with you, has he?"

Staring down at the wine she was swishing round and round in the glass, she shook her head. "I don't really expect to hear from him ever again."

"You wasted an opportunity, Laine," her father said flatly. "Brannon seemed very interested in you in the beginning, and judging by what I saw, the feeling was mutual. So what happened to change that?"

"I have no idea, Father. Now, excuse me while I check the roast I have in the oven," Laine replied, quickly leaving the room, refusing to allow him to make her feel incapable of holding a man's interest.

After a dinner enlivened little by conversation, Laine tidied the kitchen, then retired to her room. Outside, the rain still fell, though more gently now. The storm clouds had dissipated, but Laine felt almost as restless as the sky had earlier been. She stood at her window gazing out at the raindrops glistening on the glossy leaves of a magnolia tree and wishing that she hadn't met Nick at the beginning of the summer term. During the rest of the year, she was far busier and would have had less time to think about him. Tapping the tip of one forefinger against her lips, she heaved a sigh. Perhaps her father was right; perhaps she hadn't tried hard enough to be sufficiently scintillating with Nick.

"Oh, what rot," she muttered, as she swung away from the window. If she hadn't been scintillating enough for Nick, then so be it. And if her father was disappointed in her lack of appeal to the opposite sex, that was just too bad. Settling herself in the stuffed chair beside her bed, she picked up the family saga she'd been reading and proceeded to put both men right out of her mind. Very soon she became so engrossed with the fiction that she was only marginally aware of the doorbell ringing downstairs and the sound of her father's voice when he answered it.

It must have been fifteen or twenty minutes later when Thornton knocked on Laine's bedroom door, then came in. Reluctantly, she tore herself away from her book to look up.

"You'll want to come downstairs, Laine," her father announced. "We have a guest."

"Oh, yes, I guess I did hear the doorbell. Who's here?"

Thornton gave her a smug smile. "It's Nick."

A rush of excitement made her pulse race but she simply stared at her father. "Nick?" she at last repeated. "Nick Brannon?"

"Of course, Nick Brannon." Thornton surveyed her critically. "He wants to see you."

As Laine moved to the vanity to pick up her hairbrush, she tried valiantly to stem a rising excitement but without much success. She willed her hands to stop a slight trembling while she brushed her hair until it was shimmering like a golden soft cloud framing her face. There was too rosy a glow in her cheeks and too bright a sparkle in her eyes, she decided, surveying her reflection. She looked too excited, which was the opposite of how she wanted to appear—serene, calm, sophisticated enough not to be disconcerted by Nick's unexpected visit.

Rising from the vanity seat, Laine turned to Thornton and compulsively asked, "Has he decided about the grant? Is that why he's here?"

"No, no, it's not the grant," her father replied, his expression intent as he stepped toward her. "Laine, Nick's going to ask you to spend a week or so at his house on St. Simons. You'd be wise to accept his invitation. I hope you realize that."

"A week or so at his house?" she repeated disbelievingly. "With . . . with him?"

"Yes, a vacation," Thornton answered shortly. "And as I said, you'd be wise to accept."

Laine couldn't think of anything less wise. Even to contemplate spending a week alone with Nick was foolhardy. And she was amazed that her father couldn't recognize that. She shook her head, her expression perplexed. "You can't be serious? You couldn't really want me to accept his invitation?"

"That's precisely what I want."

"But, Father! I . . ."

"Laine, can't you cooperate and try to be grateful that Brannon's inviting you and cordial enough to accept his invitation?"

Laine's shoulders stiffened. "Father, I've never spent a vacation with a man. I think you'd have been horrified if I'd ever even considered it. But now you're pressing me to spend a week with Nick. Surely you can understand how dangerous that would be?"

Thornton tossed one hand in a dismissive gesture. "Dangerous? I don't see a thing dangerous about it. You've always been able to handle other young men. Why shouldn't you be able to handle Brannon?"

"Because he's not like other men I've known! He's . . . well, different."

"Don't talk nonsense. I don't see anything different about him."

Laine raised her eyes heavenward, realizing that perhaps only women could recognize Nick's dangerously magnetic personality. With a small hesitant movement of her hands, she attempted to explain the situation delicately. "Father, take my word for it, Nick is different. He's . . . aggressive. And I don't mean fresh or pushy. Maybe assertive's a better word for it. Or persuasive. Whatever. He's just not a man I'd risk spending a week with. He's too . . . attractive."

"That's the first time I've ever heard a woman complain about a man being *too* attractive." Thornton laughed.

"You're avoiding the truth," she countered, sharply. "Your concern about this grant is clouding your thinking, and I'm going to disappoint you. I'm not spending a week with Nick."

"Don't be difficult," her father said, his voice taking on a harder edge. "I think you should reconsider this."

"*No*, Father," she reiterated firmly, opening her door to step into the hallway. She glanced back. "I won't accept Nick's invitation, no matter what *you* say, and I'm going down right now to tell him that."

When Laine entered the living room, Nick was standing, removing the long-sleeved tan jacket that had shielded him from the rain. Though she managed to smile confidently at him, her gaze was riveted on the muscles of his

77

shoulders rippling beneath the cotton fabric of his cream polo shirt. A shivery thrill shot through her as, for the first time, she recognized the emotional implications of his invitation. If he indeed did ask her to spend a week with him, he wouldn't be expecting to share with her seven platonic days and nights. And the sheer knowledge that he desired her was exhilarating, especially since she had fully recognized during the past nine days the extent of her own attraction to him.

What would seven or more days and nights alone with him be like, she was wondering rather breathlessly as she joined him by the sofa, then sat down. Striving desperately to appear casual and composed, she spoke first. "I read in today's paper that your client in Savannah was acquitted. Congratulations."

With a brief nod of acknowledgment, Nick sat down beside her, not too close yet still close enough to be disconcerting. He wasted no time indulging in idle chitchat. "Because I knew your father thought I was here with a decision about the grant, I told him I'd come to invite you to spend a week or so at my house on St. Simons. Did he mention that?"

Laine nodded, then temptation made her hesitate an instant before she said, "It's very kind of you to think of asking me but I . . . I'm sorry. I can't accept. The school . . ."

"Even assistant directors are allowed vacations, aren't they?" Nick interrupted smoothly, the slight tensing of his jaw indicating he didn't mean to take no as an answer. "Your father mentioned it's been quite a while since you had one."

"Well, yes, that's true. But still . . ." She began in a firm tone. "I don't think I should give Marge only three days notice before taking off an entire week."

"Your father didn't seem to think that would be a problem," Nick informed her flatly, as if he were quite unimpressed with her excuse. "Actually, when I suggested you take two weeks, he said he was certain Marge would agree to that."

"Did he?" Laine's tone cooled perceptibly. Pretending to examine her fingernails with great care, she mentally cursed her father's interference. Because of what he had told Nick, the only reasonable excuse she'd had for declining this invitation had been snatched right out from under her. Now she didn't really know what to say. She was an abysmal liar, so she impulsively met those dark green eyes surveying her so speculatively and told the truth. "Father's probably right. Marge really wouldn't mind if I took even two weeks off. But I quite frankly think it would be unwise for me to accept your invitation."

A slight knowing smile tugged at the corners of Nick's mouth. "Unwise? What an odd choice of words. You sound more like you're *afraid* to accept my invitation. Are you afraid, Laine?"

"Of course not," she lied, then responded to his too deep perceptiveness defensively. "I'm sure you know many young women who'd do almost anything to spend two weeks on St. Simons with you. Why are you asking me? If I accept, won't you suspect I'm only doing so to please my father?"

"You assured me the need to please your father had nothing to do with our relationship," Nick countered, still smiling slightly. "Shouldn't I believe those assurances?"

"You didn't seem to believe them last week."

Broad shoulders lifted in a shrug. "That was last week. This is now."

"So you believe me?"

"Shouldn't I?"

"Heavens, why must you answer so many questions with questions?"

"Why must you?"

Laine laughed and tossed her hands up in surrender. "All right, I'm defeated. I can't expect to win a debate with an attorney, so don't answer my question, then."

"Oh, but I think I did answer just by coming here," Nick said softly, moving closer to catch her chin gently between thumb and forefinger. "But you haven't answered me."

Earnest regret set her delicate features. "I can't go to St. Simons, Nick."

His free hand gripped her waist, the tips of long fingers stroking into the incurving small of her back. He lowered his head until his lips were tantalizingly close to hers. His warm breath caressed her skin as he whispered coaxingly, "But you'd like to say yes, wouldn't you?"

"Yes," she confessed candidly, hoping he couldn't tell her heart was beating so rapidly that the pulses in her temples were pounding. "Yes, I think I would like to accept, but it would be a mistake to go and I know it. There are so many women in your life that . . ."

"You've been reading exaggerated reports in Atlanta's society columns," he chided, deliberately brushing her lips with his. "Every young woman I take to dinner is not a conquest, Laine. Actually, my work keeps me too busy for torrid entanglements. That fact alone should convince you I'm hardly a womanizer. Now you can accept my invitation."

Somehow, she was powerless to draw away from him, though an innate sense of caution was setting off danger signals in her head. She couldn't drag her gaze from the glittering intensity of his. She felt in that moment more vulnerable than she'd ever felt in her life, and crazily enough, the feeling wasn't all that unpleasant. It took considerable will power to let common sense prevail. She shook her head. "I can't say yes. I guess I'm more old-fashioned than you imagine. A casual two-week fling with a man is just not for me."

Nick released her chin to run his fingers through feathery soft hair. "There are no strings attached to this invitation, Laine. You won't be required to sign an affadavit agreeing we'll share a bed."

Blushes are always ill-timed, and hers was no exception. She could only hope that the heat she felt rising in her cheeks was only tinting them the palest pink. "I didn't expect to have to sign an affadavit," she said at last, admirably managing to keep her voice steady. "But I thought you must assume we . . ."

"Lawyers never assume anything," he corrected, tangling his fingers in her silken hair and pulling her head back slightly to trail a strand of burning kisses along the side of her neck. His hard mouth probed the hollow at the base of her throat as he murmured, "I'm asking you to St. Simons because you told me you like the island and because I think we should get to know each other better."

Laine's resolve was weakening. Though his caresses were belying the seemingly innocent words, her common sense was becoming quickly overpowered by emotions far stronger than reason. By now she was wanting him to really kiss her more than she had ever wanted anything. Perhaps he sensed that, because a mere fraction of a second later he lifted his head to cover her mouth with his, tenderly at first, then with an ever-increasing pressure that enticed her soft lips to part eagerly beneath the firmness of his. He was an aggressor capable of expertly eliciting her cooperation. When he drew her to him, she slipped slender arms around him, unresisting even as he lowered her back into the corner of the sofa. Beneath the evocative weight of his upper body, her softly cushioned breast yielded to hard muscularly contoured chest, and when the palms of his hands cupped the straining sides, brushing slowly back and forth, she instinctively arched against him.

A low murmur of satisfaction came from deep in his throat. Gentle yet demanding hands roamed freely, exploring every warm-fleshed feminine curve. Yet when he spread his fingers possessively across her flat abdomen and the tip of his tongue sought the veined softness of her inner lower lip, an intermingling of a natural fear of the unknown and awakening desires made her tremble.

"You are afraid," he muttered against her mouth, "aren't you?"

"No," she lied again, amazed she'd managed to make the denial sound convincing. "I'm not really."

"Good. You'll come with me to St. Simons, then," he stated rather than asked, his deep voice appealingly husky. "Just say yes, Laine."

"Yes." She obeyed automatically and was glad she did. She longed to spend two weeks with him and was no longer able to deny it, even to herself. Despite lingering doubts and fears, she was already too involved with Nick to let him walk away from her now. She needed to be with him.

After a last slow rousing kiss, Nick released Laine, but embers of suppressed passion glowed in his eyes as they swept over tousled blond hair and fragilely structured face. "Sometimes I think you're *too* intriguing," he whispered, raking his fingers through his own hair. "I almost forgot your father's here. And maybe it's a good thing for you he is."

The intimation wasn't lost on her. A sharp breath caught deep in her throat, but she managed a little laugh before asking, "Is that a warning, Nick?"

"It's simply a fact," he stated unabashedly, then gave her a quizzical smile. "Want to change your mind about going to the island with me?" When she shook her head in response, his smile deepened. "You still feel a little uncertain, though. Maybe it'll help to know that another couple, friends of mine, will be guests at the beach house while you're there."

"Why didn't you say so in the first place? That makes everything different," she softly exclaimed. Emotions of disappointment and relief combined, but the relief was the predominant feeling, and she was totally unaware that her admission had confirmed his guess that she was afraid to be alone with him.

"I wanted you to accept before you knew we'd be 'chaperoned' properly."

"Why?"

"It's an important enough distinction, don't you think?" he replied enigmatically, rising to his feet. After picking up his jacket, he tossed it back over one shoulder, then simply looked down at her as she stood also. Very slowly, he reached out and brushed the hair-roughened back of his hand against her cheek, but stepped away from her after only a few too-brief seconds. As they walked to the front door together, he announced abruptly, "I'll come for you Friday evening around six. All right?"

"Why don't I just drive my car down?" Laine suggested. "It's less than an hour's drive and you won't have to bother coming for me."

"And you'll have transportation in the event you want to make a fast getaway," he retorted, only half teasingly. "You don't really trust me, Laine. But maybe you'll begin to during the two weeks we're together."

She hoped so. With all her soul, she wanted to trust him completely. When he opened the door after saying good-night, she touched his arm, trailing fingertips over bare brown skin. "Thank you for asking me, Nick."

He answered by gathering her in his arms again and

taking her mouth in a brief but satisfyingly intense kiss. Then he went out into the rain-drenched night.

Laine closed the door behind him and leaned back against it. She had to be insane to have accepted his invitation. Yet the temptation had been too strong to resist. Besides, she reminded herself with a wry smile, now she wouldn't have to hear her father's complaints.

CHAPTER FIVE

Laine passed through picturesque Brunswick before seven Friday evening. After turning off U.S. 17 onto the Torras Causeway, she glanced quickly at the directions Nick had given when he'd phoned her last night. She mentally repeated the directions as she crossed the divergent channels of the intracoastal waterway. Because she had visited St. Simons Island before, she was familiar with some of the roads and didn't believe finding Nick's house would be difficult.

After passing over the last causeway bridge, Laine veered her cream Omni right onto King's Way, which curved toward the southern shore. Too quickly, it seemed, she was passing the entrance to Retreat Plantation and spotting the narrow asphalt lane Nick had told her to take. Her heartbeat accelerated to thudding rapidity. Now that she had nearly reached her destination, she wondered nervously if she should turn around and speed back home. No, she decided, with a slight uptilting of her chin. She was old enough and wise enough to spend two weeks with a man, even a man as dangerously attractive as Nick.

Her sudden case of nervous apprehension momentarily dispelled, Laine proceeded along the drive bordered by vibrant flowers. Snarled boughs of ancient live oaks, laced with Spanish moss, met overhead in a tunnel of greenery, filtering the sunlight to a few dappled patches on the asphalt. From her window she caught glimpses of secluded vacation homes, but knowing Nick's was located at the end of the road, she drove on. Soon the salt-freshened scent of the air became stronger as the road terminated in a cul-de-sac. Taking the white pebbled driveway as Nick had directed, Laine entered a copse of trees which provided permanent shade for a sprawling one-story cedar house. Beyond the house and trees stretched the sea. At the end of the driveway Laine stopped her Omni next to Nick's silver Jaguar, switched off the engine, and gazed out at the magnificent view of blue-green waters tumbling in foaming cascades onto pure white sands.

Delighted with the house and its location, Laine got out of the Omni and went around to open the trunk, but before she could take out her canvas suitcase, Nick appeared from around the corner of the house. Clad in white tennis shorts and a white shirt that accentuated his bronze skin, he strode to the car, stilling Laine's hand when she reached for her luggage. He effortlessly lifted the large suitcase, then gave her a rather mischievous grin.

"So you didn't lose your nerve," he teased. "I thought you might change your mind about coming at the last minute."

"Never crossed my mind." Hooking her thumbs into the back pockets of her own khaki shorts, Laine wrinkled her nose at him. "Well, no more than three or four times, anyhow."

As Nick draped one arm across Laine's shoulders and they walked toward the house, she smiled up at him, feeling more at ease than she ever had in his presence. Though his very casual clothing actually heightened his aura of unmistakable virility, he seemed younger in tennis attire, younger and less commanding. Laine was relieved; now she felt less as if she were balanced on the edge of a precipice.

The interior of Nick's house was as charming as the exterior. The great room with beams crisscrossing the stucco ceiling and polished hardwood floors was furnished with two rattan sofas and several chairs containing plump ice blue cushions. A plush blue area rug lay before the stone fireplace, available for use on cool evenings. Sliding glass doors opened onto a deck overlooking the beach, and Laine looked around the room, nodding obvious approval.

"I really like this," she commented, brushing her hand over the top of a sofa cushion as they passed it. "Now I understand why you'd rather live here all the time."

Nodding, Nick directed Laine down a long hallway, then stopped at the third door on the left. He opened it and followed as Laine stepped into the large bedroom. Sheer apricot curtains billowed in the breeze that drifted through open windows, and a quilted apricot spread covered the wide bed with carved mahogany headboard. While Nick placed Laine's suitcase on a carved antique chest at the foot of the bed, she placed her purse on the vanity.

"It's lovely, Nick," she complimented genuinely. "It's rare to see this many antique pieces perfectly matched."

"You can give a decorator credit for that," he replied wryly. "After I bought the bed and chest at an estate sale, she scoured the countryside for the dresser and chest and even managed to come up with the vanity and cheval glass. I never would have had the time or patience to find them myself. I'd rather spend my leisure time on the beach."

"Umm. I love the beach too," Laine said, gazing dreamily out the window. "Why don't we go for a walk now? I can hardly wait to wade in the surf again and feel the water swirling around my ankles."

"And since you have such very lovely ankles, that's a scene I look forward to watching," Nick responded with a rather wicked smile. "But we'll have to postpone our walk until after dinner, which Bob and Liz, the friends I mentioned, insisted on preparing. Come along, we don't want to keep our chefs waiting."

Laine hesitated, indicating her attire with a sweeping gesture of one hand. "Don't you think maybe I should put on a dress?"

"No." Taking Laine's left hand in his right, Nick led her toward the door. "We're on vacation, remember. Formalities don't count. You may even lounge around the house naked if you want to."

Laine laughed up at him. "Thanks for the offer but I don't have to go quite that far to be comfortable."

"Pity," he murmured, dark green eyes playing lazily over her slender, softly curved form. "But if you should change your mind . . ."

Such teasing banter made Laine feel even more relaxed. Nick in a playful mood she could handle. It was the seriously intense Nick she had to worry about.

Dinner was delightful. Liz and Bob Frederick, both in their early fourties, were friendly and interesting, and the meal they had prepared was delicious. With a main course of shrimp, bought fresh that afternoon in Brunswick, they served curried rice pilaf, salad, then fresh strawberries for dessert. But it was the congenial atmosphere that made dinner the real success. Already Laine liked the Fredericks and looked forward to spending the evening with them.

As it turned out, Liz and Bob had made other plans. After Liz and Laine tidied the kitchen they joined the men in the great room, and Bob rose from the sofa, smiling expectantly at his wife.

"Ready to go, dear?" he inquired, glancing at his wristwatch. "The Tylers expect us at nine, you know, and it's now ten till."

"We're playing bridge with the Tylers tonight. We met them on the golf course yesterday," Liz explained, speculatively eyeing Nick, then Laine, then turning to Nick again. She smiled knowingly. "You'll forgive us for leaving the two of you alone, won't you, dear?"

"You're forgiven," Nick assured her. "Laine and I planned a walk on the beach anyway."

A minute or so later, when the front door clicked shut behind the older couple as they left, a long silence commenced in the great room. After idly examining a crystal gazelle that adorned the table beside the sofa, Laine glanced up at Nick. Her breathing went all akilter as she recognized without any doubt that he was no longer in a teasing bantering mood. Narrowed eyes traveled slowly over her and every inch of her skin burned as if touched by a hot brand. And she was not yet ready to deal with the sensuously persuasive man she knew Nick could be. With the most composed smile she could muster, she stood up quickly and went to him, reaching down to take his right hand, tugging when strong fingers closed around her own.

"I'd love that walk now," she murmured, highly relieved when he nodded and rose lithely to his feet.

Outside, the light of a lemon-colored moon shone luminescently on the sea. As Laine and Nick walked toward the breaking waves, she drew in a deep breath of the fresh night air and impulsively slipped her hand around his left arm

"I like Bob and Liz," she announced, breaking the silence with an impersonal topic of conversation. "They're so nice."

"Yes, very," Nick agreed. "I thought you'd like them. They've been my friends for a long time. After I passed the bar exam, I worked in Bob's firm for over a year before establishing my own practice. But I still see both of them as often as I can."

Laine smiled up at him. "Longtime relationships are comforting, aren't they? I still keep in touch with some friends I had in elementary school. It's so much fun to talk to them. They're like family."

"Speaking of family and relationships, I think it's time we discussed your father." Halting abruptly, Nick gently gripped Laine's shoulders, turning her to face him. Behind him, the moon shimmered down, casting him in shadow, concealing his expression. His fingers stroked coaxingly as they probed her shoulders' delicate hollows and bones. "Your father's not the easiest person to be close to, is he?"

"No," she admitted, chewing her lower lip, unaware that in the pale moonlight her own expression was easily readable. Despite the weight of Nick's hands, she lifted her shoulders in a shrug. "But we get along well enough, I guess. There's certainly nothing about our relationship to justify your suspicion that he intimidates me."

Shaking his head, Nick drew her closer until his breath was stirring tendrils of her hair when he answered, "I'm not saying this to hurt you, but I did notice the change in your father's tone when he showed me that photo of your sister. He'd criticized you for having a child's handprint on your skirt but he spoke of her as if she were a perfect princess. Laine, it has to hurt when he does that."

"Maybe it did long ago but not anymore," she said stiffly, wanting no one's pity, especially his. "Now I realize Father dotes on Regina because she resembles Mother much more closely than I do. And since I can't help that and am quite satisfied with the way I look, there's no reason to brood about the way he feels. Is there?"

"Don't hide your true feelings behind that logical mind of yours. You don't have to do that with me," Nick whispered, lowering his dark head, brushing firm lips against her right temple. "The love and approval of a parent is important to anyone."

"I'm just wise enough to accept what can't be changed," she replied, forcing a smile as she pulled away from him. "Now, enough of that. I didn't come here to be psycho-analyzed. I came for a vacation, which I intend to enjoy to the fullest." With that she rushed toward the frothing surf, advancing courageously toward it when it receded, then running back laughingly to escape when it returned. It was a game from childhood but never before played when the stakes were expensive leather sandals. Yet to-night she felt reckless, reckless enough to tarry until the very last instant before retreating from the crashing waves. At last her timing was off a fraction of a second. She was caught. The ocean, patiently regular in its ageless rhythm, became the victor. Surprisingly warm water, soft with salt, rushed over sandals and toes, then swirled up-ward around Laine's ankles. She gazed down as sand shift-ed beneath her feet when the wave receded.

The moonlit surf was dazzling—a dazzling vision that intensified acutely when Nick suddenly swept her up in his arms to carry her away from the inrushing sea. With a soft murmur, his mouth descended and she succumbed to the pleasure of hard possessive lips parting her own. She wrapped her arms around his neck, and when the tip of his tongue touched each corner of her mouth, he once again awakened that aching emptiness within her. Then common sense reasserted itself. Laine resisted, pushing at his broad shoulders until he released her lips, although reluctantly, and lowered her feet to the damp sand.

He looked down at her, eyes heavily lidded. "You gam-bled with the sea, Laine," he said softly. "Are you brave enough to gamble with me?"

"Not yet," she sighed, taking a backward step to escape the nearly irresistible warmth emanating from him

To her relief, a dog, golden in the moonlight, appeared on the beach, loping in their direction, pausing momentarily here and there to splash merrily in the bubbling surf. When she spotted Nick, she raced to him, wiggling joyously before she sat down, her strong tail beating an adoring tattoo on the sand.

"Oh, isn't she lovely," Laine said enthusiastically, sinking to her knees to begin much appreciated scratching behind the animal's silken ears. "Is she yours, Nick?"

"She is. Her name's Greta, and she's mistress of this stretch of beach."

Laine smiled, then resumed scratching when big brown eyes begged and a velvety soft nose nudged her hand. Though Greta would have been content with this particular kind of petting forever, Nick adroitly distracted her by tossing a stick down the beach. When she galloped after it, he and Laine followed.

For the next half hour or so, Greta claimed most of their attention. Tirelessly, she returned with the stick for Nick to throw again and again. Then, bored with that game, she entertained them by frolicking in the surf. Barefoot this time, Laine waded in, too, laughing as the dog pounced from one swirling whirlpool of sand to another as if she really expected to find some amazing discovery in one of them. They were back almost directly in front of Nick's house when Greta spotted a large piece of driftwood just beyond them on the beach. From her throat came a deep growl and a few low gruff barks before she crouched down and slowly began to advance as if she spied her worst enemy.

When a strong arm slipped around Laine's waist and Nick directed her toward the house, she laughed up at him. "Surely she's seen driftwood before?"

"She knows what it is. It's a game she likes to play." He grinned. "She'll sneak up on it, sniff it, then run off and forget it awhile. Then when she comes back and sees it, she'll bark and start all over again."

"I could almost envy her," Laine confessed as they stepped up on the redwood deck that extended the length of the house. "Just think—she can play on the beach any time she wants and I'm only going to have two weeks."

"But the two weeks are just beginning," Nick reminded her, dropping down onto a chaise longue and drawing her down beside him. "So let's make certain we don't waste a moment of them."

Suddenly, everything was different. Gone was the light-hearted mood of only a moment ago. Now the very atmosphere seemed charged with electricity and Nick's touch electric as well, his hands smoothly spanning her waist. Close to him, lying on her side facing him on the narrow chaise, Laine quivered when those hands slipped beneath her shirt, fingertips gliding across her bare midriff. He arched her against him and, lowering his head, sought the curve of creamy smooth throat. His lips found the pulse there and she felt them curve to a smile as his mere touch increased the beat to frantic rapidity. Tense with eager anticipation, she clutched his shirtfront while he trailed tiny nibbling kisses up her neck, along the line of her jaw to the lobe of one ear. Gentle even teeth teased and tasted that morsel of flesh, and Laine shivered with the piercing thrill that shafted through her when he whispered her name. The kisses resumed, touching her temples, her eyelids, and the slight hollows of her cheeks; at last, when his mouth covered her lips, passion exploded between them. The muscular arm round her waist tautened to iron-hardness, crushing her against him while he cupped the back of her head in his free hand, holding her fast as the kiss they exchanged deepened.

"You smell delicious," he whispered roughly, fingers

grazing the rounded curve of the side of one breast. "And you feel so . . . God, I love to touch you."

". . . love to touch you too," she murmured, nearly incoherent in her breathlessness. With her words her slender arms slid beneath his shirt. Her hands played over his broad smooth back, fingers tracing the contours of corded muscles. Nick shuddered, and with a low growl of desire, his lips hardened, exerting an exquisite twisting pressure. The soft shape of her lips clung to his as she responded, her mouth opening wider, inviting the invading thrust of tongue that tasted the sweetness within.

Though Laine seemed to melt against him, she didn't feel close enough even yet. The fingers of one hand tangled in the springy hair on his nape, urging with slight pressure a rougher taking of her mouth. He complied, devouring her lips, catching the tender bottom curve between his teeth to tug open her mouth even wider to the marauding seduction of his. Blazing desire rushed the blood through her veins, overheating her skin until she felt almost faint with dizzying sensations.

Only the whisper of a breeze rustling the trees' leaves, the rhythmic rush of the ocean, and their own irregular breathing disturbed the night silence, and with Nick, Laine felt lost in a world no one else could share. She offered no resistance even when he deftly undid the buttons of her shirt and removed it, allowing it to drop with a swish to the floor beside the chaise. Then, when her lace bra joined the shirt on the floor, she could only breathe a soft sigh, signaling acquiescence. Drowsily, through the fringe of thick lashes, she watched with half-closed eyes as his strong, tan hands moved toward her breasts, whose rapid rise and fall accelerated perceptibly as he caressed with a warm, sure touch. Pleasantly rough fingertips traced the ivory smooth skin round and round until every sloping inch had been kindled into a consuming fire.

By the time Nick closed his mouth around one swollen peak then the other, possessing her with moist pulling pressure, she was moaning softly, every nerve ending exquisitely receptive, her breathing shallow. Nick's breathing, too, was uneven when his mouth covered hers again to plunder soft pliant lips.

With trembling fingers she unbuttoned his shirt, her palms easing over his warm, smooth skin with torturing slowness. She savored the feel of him, the very scent and taste of him. Moving her mouth from his, she ran her tongue down the sweep of his neck and muscular shoulder, then up again, circling his ear until he groaned, an utterly masculine, uninhibited sound of pleasure that aroused her even further.

Inexperienced as she was, Laine could not help but respond to Nick's nearness; she had never felt the kind of intoxicating exhilaration that now seemed to rule her, to compel her to lovingly explore the contours of his hard muscular body. He was like a drug to her senses, a drug she could never get enough of. His deep sighs made her realize with stunning clarity how very right it felt to be in his arms, how much she wanted their lovemaking to go on and on.

Endearments whispered close to her ear accompanied the swift unfastening of the snap on her waistband and the subsequent lowering of her shorts' zipper. Laine gasped as his hand slipped beneath the khaki fabric and glided possessively across her flat abdomen. Through the fabric of her panties, his skin scorched her own, but though his touch was an unbelievable pleasure, she tensed when his hand slid downward. She caught his wrist and brought that hand back upward to her waist, where she held it still.

"*Nick,*" she breathed, fighting her desire and his as she pulled away from him. Her eyes flickered open as his did and she felt impaled by the gleam of passion ablaze in the green depths. Yet, she resisted the need to surrender to him. Innate caution and a wariness ingrained after years of standing on the sidelines combined to strengthen self-restraint. She took a deep breath. "I . . . it's late. It's time for bed, don't you think?"

"God, I hope that's an invitation," he muttered huskily, his jaw hardening as she shook her head. There was more than a hint of reluctance in his arms as he released her. "Then run away, Laine."

She scrambled up from the chaise and he lay back on it, one arm upflung to cover his eyes. Gathering her clothes up from the deck's planking, she wanted to say something, anything, to him but could think of nothing to say that would suffice. At last, she brushed a hand over his in silent apology and rushed inside, across the darkened great room, and down the long hall to her lonely bed.

The next two days were a delight. Nick was a man who knew how to play, and Laine remembered how, just by being with him. They enjoyed a couple of games of tennis, though she was no match for him, but most often they were swimming or just lounging on the beach. They walked miles along the sand, usually with Greta gamboling along beside them, and their topics of conversation were endlessly varied. Nothing about Nick was ever boring. Laine liked everything about him; in fact, by the end of the second full day, she knew that the liking was swiftly, inexorably becoming loving. She was falling in love with him and was powerless to do anything to prevent it, which made it increasingly more difficult to resist whenever they touched, accidentally or otherwise, and couldn't stop touching. With every fiber of her being Laine sensed Nick's growing frustration each time she forced herself to draw away before surrender became inevitable. Yet she had to resist. She was in love and needed love in return, something he might never be able to give. So the battle of wills continued, and she could only be grateful the Fredericks were staying at the house. Though she and Nick spent little time with them, their mere presence was reassuring, especially during the nights.

For that reason the news she heard Monday morning came as quite a surprise and an upset. After breakfast, while the two women were tidying the kitchen, Liz claimed Laine's complete attention when she breathed a long dismayed sigh.

"Sometimes I really dislike Bob's profession," she explained with a resigned smile. "There's so little time to relax, and I resent that. It seems there's always some pressing case he has to attend to. I do wish we didn't have to go back to Atlanta today. I especially wanted to get better acquainted with you."

Laine felt rooted to the spot. "You mean you're . . . leaving here today?"

"Pity, isn't it? I wish we didn't have to go, but Bob says we must get back."

"Maybe you can visit again soon. You're welcome back here any time. You know that, Liz," Nick said from the doorway, shifting a dark unreadable gaze immediately to Laine. He stepped into the kitchen as Liz was leaving it, shaking her head and patting his arm in passing.

For several seconds Laine's thoughts found no voice as indignation rose in her, unfurling scarlet flags of color in her cheeks. Posture stiff and unyielding, chin outthrust, she at last muttered, "I can hardly believe this. That you would plan deliberately to . . ."

"I planned nothing," Nick interrupted tersely, taking one long step to eliminate the distance between them, practically cornering Laine between cabinets and the outside kitchen door. Placing a hand on the wall on each side of her—in effect, trapping her there—he met the resentment in her blue eyes unflinchingly. "I didn't know until a few minutes ago that Bob and Liz were leaving. He received an urgent call early this morning and decided they must leave today."

"Is that true?" she questioned sharply, longing to believe him yet afraid to. "Is it, Nick?"

"You seem to be forgetting you agreed to come here *before* I ever mentioned Bob and Liz. And since you did, I had no reason to manufacture an elaborate lie, did I?"

Caught somewhat off balance by that indisputable truth, Laine thoughtfully nibbled the side of her upper lip, a tiny frown marring her brow. "Oh, I don't know what to think now. It just seems so convenient that . . ."

"Do you want to go running home then?" he asked bluntly, impatience hardening his chiseled features. "I won't stop you from going, you know. But I find it hard to believe you really think I tricked you into coming here. Do you?"

"No, I guess I really don't," she admitted, suspicion slowly dying though a few lingering doubts remained. "But still . . ."

"*Laine,*" he murmured, moving closer, cupping her neck in a large yet gentle hand, his thumbs lifting her chin. His voice lowered, became more deeply coaxing, almost seductive in timbre. "You wanted to come here before you knew about Bob and Liz, so what difference does it make now that they have to leave?"

Laine gazed up at him, nearly mesmerized by his deeply resonant tone, the soft light in his eyes, and the fingertips that were playing havoc with her senses as they slowly brushed back and forth along the line of her jaw. The situation was different now. She was in love with him, which made their being alone together infinitely more dangerous. But she could hardly tell him that. Such an admission would only serve to embarrass him and humiliate her.

"I suppose I just got used to having the Fredericks around," she said instead. "But if they have to leave, that's just the way it is."

"So you'll stay anyway?"

"Yes," she whispered, unable to abide the thought of leaving him, though she knew what she was risking with her decision. "I'll stay."

"I wonder why," he whispered back, searching her face with a serious intensity that nearly took her breath away. Then he released her and stepped away. "Maybe you'll feel more comfortable, though, if we spend our evenings with some of the couples I know on the island?"

"That sounds like a nice idea," she answered, trying not to sound too relieved. "I think I'll like meeting new people."

"We'll see," was his noncommittal answer, but judging from the icy green glint in his eyes, he was far from pleased. And in that moment, the tension they had nearly managed to eliminate during the past two days closed in on them. To Laine it seemed almost like a heavy curtain of mist falling between them.

CHAPTER SIX

Nick had planned it. He *must* have. Laine truly suspected he had deliberately arranged to have dinner Monday evening with the most boring couple he knew. Within minutes after meeting Thad and Joyce Brice, Laine realized it was going to be an excruciatingly long evening. Though Laine herself was reasonably impressed by the most famous restaurant on Sea Island, that resort mecca located directly east of St. Simons, Joyce Brice acted as if she had died and gone to heaven. Although she repeatedly assured Laine that she and her husband regularly dined at the Priory, she belied those assurances by practically squealing every time she spotted a movie star or politician, or even one of the better-known local gentry. Worst of all, at one point she actually flitted from table to table, eliciting some irritated glances from notables who, after all, had chosen to stay at the Priory for its acclaimed privacy. They were seeking escape from people like Joyce Brice. To no avail. There she was, swooping from table to table like a noisy, gawking seabird.

Laine was embarrassed, especially so when Joyce returned to their table and proceeded to gossip about people who were seated no more than a few yards away. Unfortunately, her husband, Thad, seemed amused by her insipid chatter and even encouraged it. All in all, it was the dullest meal Laine had ever endured. She glanced often at Nick, whose expression remained completely inscrutable. Surely he was being bored to death too.

At last the meal ended, and while Joyce Brice craned her neck this way and that to better ogle famous faces, Nick mercifully asked Laine to dance.

"Oh, yes, let's do," she said, unable to suppress an audible sigh of relief. It was a relief that would be short-lived. The moment Nick placed his arm round her waist and they began dancing, she knew that a barrier was still there between them, as it had been all day. Laine sighed, but Nick gave no indication that he noticed. It was a silent dance, and the touch of Nick's hands was impersonal until, when the music ended, he draped an arm across her shoulders almost companionably as they walked back to their table.

"Well, Laine," he murmured, looking down at her. "Having a good time?"

"Dandy," she shot back, pretending she didn't notice the trace of amusement that lifted the corners of his sensuously shaped mouth.

By midnight Laine was finding it necessary to hide a succession of yawns behind her hand as Joyce Brice chattered on incessantly. Finally, when Laine felt sure she would soon fall asleep in her chair, Nick took pity on her and ended her misery—and his own. As Nick drove her back across the causeway to St. Simons, he had very little to say. When they arrived home, however, he did take her hand in his as they walked to the house. But once inside, to her disappointment, he released it and went to the bar to pour himself a drink. When she declined his invitation to join him, he stood, one elbow resting on the bar, watching over the rim of his glass as she prowled restlessly around the great room.

"Something wrong, Laine?" he queried, his tone unusually sardonic. "You don't seem able to relax. Surely you're not still worried about being here alone with me? After I've done my best all day to convince you that you have nothing to fear?"

"Oh, is that what you've been doing?" Stopping behind one sofa, she smiled wryly. "And I thought maybe you were just getting tired of me." When he neither returned the smile nor answered, she sighed. "Oh, okay, maybe I did give you the wrong impression this morning. I'm sorry if I seemed not to trust you. I really think I do, you know."

"When you decide for certain, let me know," he answered, darkened eyes boring into her as he put his glass down on the bar. "Right now, maybe you should go to bed, since we plan to go sailing early in the morning."

Though it was an obvious dismissal, Laine hesitated, unhappiness gathering in a knot in her chest as she realized how futile it would be to try to explain feelings she didn't understand herself. One thing she did understand was that Nick was finding her uncertainty frustrating and boring. And the last thing she wanted to do was bore him. Drawing herself up to her full height, which wasn't considerable, she returned his gaze steadily, self-protective coolness graying her eyes as she simply asked outright, "Maybe you'd rather I just go home tomorrow?"

Nick's expression didn't alter. "Is that what you want to do?"

"Is that what you'd like me to do?"

"Laine, for God's sake!" he nearly growled, straightening by the bar, lean body so taut he reminded her of a tiger poised to spring. "For once, can't you say what *you* want? Do you want to go home tomorrow or don't you?"

She shrugged. "That depends. If I'm boring you . . ."

"This conversation is boring me, but you never do," he muttered, thrusting his hands deep in his pockets. "How could you possibly bore me when I never know what to expect from you?"

"I never know what to expect from you, either," she retorted, appealing pink color tinting her cheeks. "You're a very . . . unpredictable man."

"Then that's settled—we don't bore each other. Now, about tomorrow, do you want to go or stay?"

"Do you want me to stay?"

Muttering an oath beneath his breath, he started toward her, his expression menacing. "There's a limit to my patience, Laine, and I don't intend to stand here all night waiting for you to tell me what *you* want to do."

"All right then, yes," she said calmly, glad he couldn't know how her heartbeat quickened when he stopped close in front of her. Looking up at him, she forced herself to ignore the dawning realization that he was even more dangerous than she had imagined him to be. Smoldering beneath the surface of cool deliberate control was a wealth of emotions that she instinctively knew ran deep. She got the distinct impression it would take no more than one wrong word from her, or even a touch, to release searing passions that would quickly consume both of them. Overwhelmingly aware of his latent power and her own extreme vulnerability, she carefully chose her words, "I would like to stay, Nick. That's what *I* want to do. And you're right, it's late. I think I'll go to bed now. Goodnight."

She started to step around him, then gasped softly when her right wrist was captured in an iron-hard grip. Her eyes darted up to meet his and darkened with confusion when he gave her an unexpectedly indulgent smile.

"There's something you should know, Laine," he said very softly. "I'm not going to make this decision for you by seducing you, despite your uncertainty. In my bed, I

103

want a woman who knows what she wants and why she wants it, a woman who's more than willing. Understand?"

"Such a blunt summation of your requirements, counselor," she replied tersely, somehow managing not to blush. "I'd have to be rather dense not to understand exactly what you mean. And I'll certainly keep what you said in mind."

With that show of bravado, she resolutely extricated her wrist from the strong fingers which held it, then proceeded down the hallway at a slow leisurely pace she hoped would convince him he hadn't disconcerted her in the least. Once in her room, however, with the door closed behind her, she flung herself across the wide bed, nuzzling her cheek against the coverlet. So Nick wanted total abandon from her and she wanted love from him. An impossible situation, she thought bleakly, knowing they could probably never reconcile such different needs.

When dusk faded into darkness Wednesday evening, Chinese lanterns illuminated the small garden party of Nick's friends, Walt and Joan Bennett. Seated on a bench in the rose arbor, Laine breathed in the sweet scent and smiled contentedly at Nick as he approached. When he presented her with a glass of white wine, she took it but wrinkled her nose in a slight grimace. "I really shouldn't have this, you know. I've already had two glasses since we got here."

"You've also had dinner. But if you'd rather not have it . . ."

"I'll just take a sip now and then," she told him as he joined her on the bench, placing the tumbler of Scotch and water he'd brought for himself on the wrought-iron table beside him. For a moment he sat silently, arms resting on his thighs, hands hanging loosely between his knees as he looked out at the few guests milling over the flagstone patio. Suddenly, he turned to look at Laine, then reached around her to pluck a perfect crimson rosebud from its bed of green foliage clinging to a white lattice. After snapping off an excess of stem and removing a tiny thorn, he slipped the flower into Laine's hair, above her left ear, smiling when she touched gentle fingertips to the velvety petals.

"Are you having a better time tonight?" he asked quietly. "How do you like the Bennetts?"

"Oh, they're very nice and very interesting. Joan is a volunteer in the local elementary school, so of course we had a great deal to talk about."

"How tactful you are not to compare the Bennetts with the Brices," he teased, laughing as she lifted her eyes heavenward in remembrance. "I agree with that assessment completely and I want to apologize for asking them to have dinner with us. Actually, I'd never met Joyce before last night, so I didn't know she was so . . ."

"Flamboyant?"

"Silly is a better description," he amended bluntly. "And I'm sorry it was such a dull evening."

"I've been trapped with duller people, I assure you, and for longer periods of time. And besides, now we're even," Laine said with a wry smile. "I introduced you to Dulcie Jacobs. Remember? She's a lot like Joyce Brice except she talks constantly about the arts committees she's on instead of about celebrities. Actually, I feel sort of sorry for both of them. They try so hard to seem important. I imagine Mrs. Brice spent all of today telling people she had dinner last night with the famous attorney Nick Brannon."

"She's welcome to tell the entire world if she likes, as long as I never have to spend time with her again," Nick said seriously. "Status seeking is a very unattractive trait, one for which I have no patience."

"I'll remember that," Laine quipped. "In case I'm ever tempted to act like Dulcie or Joyce around you."

"That'll never happen. There's nothing in you like either of those women," he replied, solemnly examining her upturned face. "Maybe you don't realize it, Laine, but there's something about you that makes you seem very wise for your years."

Laine grimaced. "My, that makes me sound like an awful dullard."

"No, love, it makes you an intriguing mystery," Nick whispered, brushing a wayward strand of hair back from her cheek, allowing his fingertips to linger against creamy skin. "You present a challenge most men would find hard to resist. I know I do."

"A challenge? Me?" She laughed lightly. "Oh, come now, I bet you say that to all the girls."

"You lose your bet then," he murmured, stilling her laughter at once when his fingertips drifted downward into the shadowed hollow between her breasts, seeking bare skin beneath the bodice of her low-cut dress. "I've never said that to anyone else because no woman's ever been the mystery to me that you are, Laine." Fingertips feathered her breastbone; knuckles pressed gently into rounded flesh. "What fiery emotions are you hiding in there? That's what I have to find out."

Laine shook her head, dragging herself back from the warm weakening lethargy his huskily spoken words and grazing touch had induced. "Nick, I . . ."

"Dance with me," he commanded softly, taking her hand to draw her to her feet. And when she glided obediently into his arms, he held her close to him, his lips moving over the silken cap of moon-silvered hair.

In the rose-scented cool night air, beneath a starry sky, every beat of the music became a senuous pulsation. Laine's arms slipped up around Nick's neck as both his encircled her waist. In that evocative embrace they remained in the secluded arbor, simply swaying slightly to a slow seductive rhythm. Nuzzling her cheek into the warm hollow of his shoulder, she relaxed. The graceful curving contours of her slender body were molded into the firmer line of his, and she delighted in the feel of potent masculinity.

It was as if they were alone in the world, and when Nick's lips touched her left temple, she lifted her face to gaze drowsily up at him. "Aren't you ever going to kiss me again?" she whispered compulsively. "It's been two days, and I . . ."

"God, I know how long it's been!" he whispered back. Then he was seeking, finding, taking her mouth with a rough demand that brooked no denial.

As if she could have denied him. The instant his hardening lips took possession of hers, she stretched up on tiptoe, kissing him back, tightening her arms around his neck and pressing against him, unable to get close enough.

The tenor of his breathing altered, became nearly as quickly drawn as hers, while his hands at her sides followed the line of hip to the enticing insweep of her waist and upward to linger, palms cupping the soft firm curves of her breasts. His mouth plundered the sweetness of hers again and again. Laine responded with complete abandon, telling him with the touch of her lips on his, with her caress, with her soft moans of desire, that she wanted him, needed to be close to him in every way. But as suddenly as the kisses had begun, they ended. Hands on her hips, he put her away from him.

"This is crazy," he muttered. "There are people all around."

"Take me home then," she replied immediately.

"Are you sure that's really what you want?" he asked and when she nodded, his hands around her waist tightened fiercely. Almost pensive, he looked down at her for several seconds. Then a hint of a smile played over his mouth and he brought one hand up to stroke her tousled hair. "We'll have to say goodnight to the Bennetts before we go."

After that courtesy had been attended to and Nick and Laine were in his car going south, she sat close to him, resting her head against his chest. As if entranced, she could think of nothing except the arm around her shoulders, the touch of the fingers brushing her bare upper arm, and the warmth of his body radiating into her own. She almost felt dizzy and closed her eyes to the sight of the trees streaming past on each side of the road, like the flash of scenes in a dream.

They were at Nick's so soon she could hardly believe they had traveled nine miles. And it was when he got out of the car and came around to open her door that realization dawned. The magnitude of what she was inviting was an astonishment, and she might have hesitated had Nick's grip on her hand not been so firmly insistent. As they walked to the house, he slipped an arm around her waist, pulling her to his side. He said nothing, and she would always remember that in that moment all she heard was the strange repetitive music of the katydids and the sound of her own heart beating in her ears.

When Nick led Laine around the house to the deck overlooking the beach, she thought she had gained at least a temporary reprieve. She relaxed somewhat, but then her heart seemed to soar up into her throat when he immediately started to take her into his arms. Stepping back, she gestured nervously and promptly latched onto the first thought that popped into her mind.

"I'll just go put my wrap in my room and be right back," she said weakly, then gasped as the cream crocheted stole was pulled off her shoulders and tossed unceremoniously onto a deck chair. Fires blazed on her skin when gentle fingers slowly pushed aside the straps of her dress.

"Oh, no, Laine, you're not going to your room, where you can have second thoughts. You're staying here," he murmured, hands spanning her waist to pull her to him. "What you start, you have to finish."

"But I . . ."

He placed a finger to her mouth to silence her, then began a devastating assault on her senses by tracing the soft shape of her lips with his fingertip. His other hand skimmed around her waist, his touch so lightly caressing that she trembled with quickening sensations of delight. When he bent down to scatter lingering kisses over smooth shoulders, she tilted her head back, exposing the slender column of her neck to firm searching lips.

She ached for him to seek her mouth, but he didn't, though her lips were parted invitingly with her swiftly drawn breaths. Instead, he tormented her with tiny shattering nibbles at the lobes of her ears and brief electric touches of the tip of his tongue in the hollows just beneath. Laine's hands, clenched and trapped between them against his chest, slowly opened, her fingers stroking taut muscle and, after shakily undoing two buttons, slipping inside his shirt to graze over hair-roughened skin.

His hands wandered over her, shaping each curve with a deliberate lightness that further inflamed her senses. At last, when he arched her against him and touched his lips first to one corner of her mouth then the other, again again, she could stand it no longer. One hand cupped the back of his head, her fingers tangling in thick hair.

"Nick, please," she whispered, desperate for the fierce demand of his kiss. When his mouth did cover her own, she moved closer to him, but his lips only teased, brushed, played with hers until she breathed imploringly, "Oh, *Nick!*"

Widening his stance, he caught her closer to him, one hand seeking the gentle swell of her hips, pressing her against the hard lines of his body. At last his kiss became impassioned, and she gave a little murmur of satisfaction when firm lips caught her own, exerting an ever-increasing pressure that was almost bruising in intensity. So enraptured was she by the demanding hardness of his mouth that she didn't realize he had adroitly lowered the zipper of her dress until the night air caressed her bare back. By then it was too late.

"Nick," she protested softly. "*No.*"

"Yes. Oh, yes, Laine."

"But we're outside. Someone might be . . ."

"Hush," he whispered. "No one's around. It's a private beach, and I want to see you out here in the moonlight."

She tried without success to still the hands that brushed the straps of her ankle-length cream eyelet dress down her arms. She had made it so easy for him because when the bodice dropped down, the built-in bra went with it and immediately she was standing before him, bare to the waist. Instinct made her start to cover her breasts with her arms but Nick caught her wrists, preventing that protective gesture and also allowing the dress to slip through his fingers to float down around her feet. Then she stood unresisting, as if hypnotized, as he expertly removed both her long half-slip and the last remaining article of her clothing. He stepped back to look at her.

"You're so beautiful, Laine," he said huskily, gaze narrowing as it swept slowly over the gracefully sweeping lines of her slender curved body. As if he were studying a lovely work of art, he surveyed her for what seemed to her like an eternity.

She was trembling but not from cold. Heat was rushing

through and over her. No man had ever seen her naked before and an overpowering feeling of vulnerability made her legs go weak. Suddenly, as if he could no longer resist touching skin that shimmered opalescently in the moonlight, Nick moved close again, reaching out to trail his fingers over the upper curve of her breasts, then cup their weight in his hands.

Unable to withstand his burning appraisal any longer, she moved swiftly into his arms in an attempt to hide her nakedness. And when he pulled her to him, hands drifting over her delicately structured back, she knew the right of possession was his. He swept her up in his arms to carry her inside the house.

In Nick's room, he threw back the coverlet on his bed and lowered Laine gently onto the mattress. She lay very still on the cool percale sheet, watching spellbound as he quickly stripped. In the soft glow from a small lamp across the room his skin shone like burnished bronze. Involuntarily, her gaze flickered over him, over the broad strength of his shoulders, hard, subtly muscled chest, down to tapered waist, lean hips, and long powerful legs. As a woman, she found him intriguingly magnificent; as an inexperienced bedmate, she was apprehensive, somewhat intimidated by such obvious virility. Then he came down onto the bed beside her and simply held her for several minutes, lean fingers stroking, massaging her back to ease her tension.

She began to relax, and as her body went warm and pliant in the circle of his arms, she looked up at him, her love for him expanding to infinity when she recognized tenderness softening the hot glint of desire in his green eyes. He smiled, almost indulgently. And when she brushed one finger over his lips and he gently caught the tip between his teeth, she smiled back. He kissed her.

He was so patient. Obviously exercising firm control

111

over his own desires, he proceeded to arouse hers to feverish intensity. Slow, long, deepening kisses claimed her mouth as hands moved over her body in intimate exploration. His lips followed the paths blazed by his hands, seeking the round firmness of her breasts, the satiny skin of her abdomen, and the creamy smoothness of lightly tanned slender thighs.

Responsive to every caressing touch and kiss, her own hands and lips were eagerly exploring him. She delighted in his passionate sigh of pleasure, eager to give back in full measure the tender, exquisite delight he gave her. When he finally moved above her, arching her to him, her small cry soon altered to a long shuddering sigh of ecstasy. The fingers that had pressed hard into the corded muscles of his shoulders as he took her relaxed, began stroking his back.

"Laine," he groaned triumphantly, possessively. "You are a delight."

Her thumbs brushed over the strong tendons of his neck. Her lips found the rapidly beating pulse in his throat and lingered there as he moved slowly, gently, making her completely his. Her entire being throbbed to life as she merged with him.

"Oh Nick, I . . ." She never said the words, but she gave her love without hesitation. And with each slow rousing movement of his hard body, that love deepened as she was swept up in a whirlwind of passion. In his quest to give her pleasure, he conquered all her inhibitions and carried her upward in a tide of ecstasy so devastating that she cried out his name when piercing fulfillment cascaded in hot pulsating waves inside her. The throbbing ripples receded but the warmth remained, and she clung to him as he took his own satisfaction with a compelling urgency, no longer capable of gentleness.

Afterward, Laine lay wrapped in Nick's arms, her head

nestled in the hollow of his shoulder. Beneath her hand on his chest, his heart had slowed to a strong steady beat and his relaxed warm nearness was as emotionally satisfying as their lovemaking had been physically. Laine had no regrets. She had given love and he had given tender desire, and for the moment that was enough to make her content. He did feel affection for her; she could sense that and could only hope that the affection would eventually become love.

Drowsy, Laine snuggled closer to Nick, and when he began to play idly with strands of her tousled hair, she tilted her head back to look at him.

"You seduced me after all, you know, Nick," she accused teasingly.

"Ah, but you were so much more than willing," he countered huskily, smiling as a faint blush tinted her cheeks.

Dropping the veil of thick lashes over her eyes, she concealed the love she thought must be revealed in their depths. But as Nick's hand curved around her upper arm, his fingertips beginning to trace small circles on her skin, she smiled slightly to herself. It was nearly impossible to believe that she had known him for only a brief time. He had become so important to her that she felt as if he'd always been an integral part of her life. In her sleepiness, her mind began to wander. How strange destiny could be . . . If Nick's uncle hadn't been ill . . . If Nick hadn't had doubts about the grant . . . Her musing triggered a succession of interrelated thoughts until at last the special-education classroom she wanted so badly came into her mind. Half asleep, she lifted a hand to touch light fingertips to Nick's lean cheek.

"Nick," she murmured, "you are going to give Latham the grant, aren't you?" And she would have given the world to have been able to recall the words the instant they were out of her mouth and she felt him go tense beside her. Her eyes flew open and she saw the implacable set of his strong jaw and the muscle ticking with ominous regularity there. The planes of his face were now forebodingly hard beneath her fingers, and she moved her hand away in a futile gesture of apology. "Nick, I didn't mean . . ."

"I knew virginity was a rare commodity these days," he muttered through clenched teeth. "But I had no idea you'd put a million-dollar price tag on yours."

"Nick, please listen. I . . ."

"Anything for 'Father.' Right?" His voice was low, his tone harsh. "Right?"

"No, that isn't right!" she said urgently, feeling his anger in the taut inflexible line of his body, feeling her own heart react to that anger with wild palpitations. Sensing danger, she tried desperately to explain that she'd been half asleep and the question had just popped into her mind.

"Don't bother talking, Laine. We have no time for that," he interrupted her midsentence, in no mood to listen. With awesome swiftness he turned over, imprisoning her beneath him, his weight pressing her into the softness of the mattress. His eyes glittered icily as his gaze raked over her face. "A million dollars," he muttered, "hmm? Well, now that I know what a high price I'm expected to pay, I think I should get my money's worth, don't you agree?"

Laine gasped, her face going pale as a hard knee thrust downward and parted her legs, and when she faced, for the first time in her life, the proof of a man's overwhelming physical superiority, she panicked. She threw her hands against his broad chest, pushing as she frantically twisted beneath him. But her struggle for freedom was useless. Catching both her wrists in one large hand, Nick pushed

114

her arms back on the pillow and one long muscular leg pinned hers beneath it. Held practically immobile, completely in his power, she moved her head from side to side on the pillow, but if he noticed the hurt and growing apprehension in her widening eyes, he gave no indication of it.

Despair chilled Laine to the bone, and when Nick's free hand stroked across her abdomen and upward to cup one breast, she flinched and whispered imploringly, "Please, Nick, don't let it be like this. If you force me . . ."

"I don't intend to force you," he said flatly. "I won't have to."

He was right. He slowly seduced her, and when his hands began to move over her in insistent sweeps and his tongue opened her mouth to a succession of possessive marauding kisses, her body traitorously responded. She lost all will to resist, unable to contain the love she felt for him. He had released her arms, and she wrapped them around his waist as their bodies merged again.

He immersed himself in her. Yet, despite his anger, despite the misconception, he was no less gentle, no less considerate than he had been before. Letting the fires of his own passion smolder, with slow deliberation he transported her to the peak of ecstasy again and again until she felt faint with the shattering sensations he brought to life within her. Then she was whispering his name, urging him nearer, compelling him to take from her as much pleasure as he had given.

Even in the aftermath, he wouldn't release her completely. Turning her onto her side as he turned also, he drew her close back against him, one arm draped possessively around her waist, his body curved around hers.

"You're mine, Laine," he whispered hoarsely into her ear. "A bargain, even at the price you're asking."

Afloat in a fulfillment that far surpassed any of her virginal expectations, she was without the energy even to try to explain to him again. Her eyelids fluttered shut, but as she drifted into sleep she was thinking he was right about one thing. She was irrevocably his.

CHAPTER SEVEN

The next morning Laine awoke alone in the bed. Sunlight streaming through the open slats of the shuttered window produced a geometric pattern on the floor in front of it and she lay still awhile as her eyes adjusted to the brightness. At last she shifted her position slightly, and with the feel of the sheet gliding over bare skin came the realization that she was totally unclothed. The night came back in a rush of memories, both erotic and disturbing, and with a soft moan she nuzzled her cheek against Nick's pillow, detecting the faint scent of him that still lingered there. A constrictive ache gathered in her chest. How could she have responded to him with such absolute abandon, knowing he believed what she had given in love had really been a bribe? *How could she have?*

Unable to answer that question, she burrowed her face deeper into Nick's pillow. Twirling a strand of hair round and round on one finger, she instinctively curled up in a self-protective ball in the center of the bed, as if she sought security by assuming the position in which she had slept as a child. That didn't help, so she stretched out her legs again while absently continuing to twirl her hair. It almost seemed she could still feel the burning imprint of Nick's hands on her body, and she knew without a doubt that he had etched his mark indelibly on her consciousness. If only he loved her half as much as she loved him.

. . . But he didn't, and she was afraid to show the true depths of her feelings and risk devastating rejection. Yet somehow she needed to convince him that her response last night hadn't been for her father's benefit, that what she had given hadn't been a bribe.

Caught up as she was in pensive thought, she was startled by the sudden sound of the door opening. She squeezed her eyes shut as every muscle in her froze and she could scarcely force herself to turn over and open her eyes again, even when Nick softly called her name.

Yet, she did it, groaning inwardly with the little catch in her heart that came when she found him standing by the bed, clad only in a short navy bathrobe. He looked too good to her, and though she ached to touch him she suppressed that desire, sensing an odd tension in him. His expression was unreadable, and when she could detect no hint of tenderness for her in it, tears that needed badly to be shed gathered hotly behind her eyes.

"I've made us some coffee," he finally announced, his deep voice devoid of emotion as he inclined his head toward the tray he'd placed on the bedside table. "And I remembered to bring sugar for yours."

For some reason, that small consideration nearly snapped the fragile control she held on her emotions. Unable to look at him any longer, afraid she might recognize contempt in his stony features, she turned her face back into the pillow. She wouldn't allow herself to cry, however—she hadn't cried in years—but the sheer effort of damming the tears that threatened to flow made her entire body begin to shake.

"For God's sake, Laine," he muttered roughly as he sat down on the edge of the bed. A hand descended on her shoulder, warm even through the sheet. "Don't cry."

"I'm not crying," she said, her voice muffled. "I never cry."

"What's wrong then? Why the trembling?" His voice gentled. "Laine, I didn't take anything from you last night you didn't want to give."

She lifted her head to stare at him, her eyes clouding with self-disdain and some resentment. "Don't you think I know that, Nick?" she asked woodenly. "How do you think it makes me feel to remember how . . . eagerly I responded, even knowing that you thought . . . think that I'm little better than a . . ."

"Quiet!" he uttered harshly, the fingers curved over her shoulder pressing down to delicate bone. He turned her over onto her back, cupping her face in one hand, forcing her to meet his piercing gaze. "You're exaggerating my reaction. Oh, I'll admit I was angry, but . . ."

"Angry! You were furious, Nick, and absolutely unwilling to listen when I tried to explain that my question had just been horribly ill-timed." She laid a small hand on the sleeve of his robe. "Really, Nick, I was just half asleep and my mind wandered, and all of a sudden I just found myself asking about the grant. I certainly didn't mean that I expected you to give it simply because we . . . our relationship had changed. Why can't you believe that?"

"I shouldn't have said what I did," he declared softly, evading her question. "My remarks were crass and unnecessary, and I apologize for them."

Lowering her gaze, Laine was unable to prevent the slight wobbling of her chin. Tears filled her eyes, obscuring her vision as she plucked miserably at the bedspread, but she blinked them away before Nick tilted her chin upward again. A saddened resigned half smile trembled on her lips. "So you still don't believe me? You really think I could . . ."

"Hell, I don't know what I think," he muttered, stroking his fingertips across her cheek. "I only know I shouldn't have said what I did."

To escape his touch, Laine sat up, tucking the sheet over her breasts under her arms to secure it, unaware that in doing so she created an enchanting décolleté drape. Nick, however, made her immediately aware of her provocative state of undress. Eyes, narrowed to green slits, swept lazily over the length of her shapely body, outlined against the bedcoverings, and lingered with breathtaking intensity on her breasts. When he slowly reached out to trace his fingers over the beginning swell and down into the hint of cleavage exposed above the sheet, conflicting desires warred within her. His caresses were so arousing—she felt at once vibrantly and wholly alive—yet for the moment the instinct for self-preservation overcame even physical need.

"I think maybe I should just leave today," she said almost inaudibly, then shivered with unbidden delight as fingers brushed over warm firm flesh. She steeled herself to the tumultuous effect his touch was having on her senses and continued, "I mean, considering the doubts you have about me and my motive for being here, I think it will be best for me to go away. Don't . . . don't you agree?"

"Not at all. I think you should stay and prove all my doubts wrong. Prove you need me as much as I need you," he whispered coaxingly. "Stay, Laine."

Though she shook her head, resolve was fading fast. A soft defeated moan escaped her as he loosened the sheet, allowing it to drop down round her waist. His large warm hands covered full creamy-fleshed breasts. When the nipples surged to tingling erectness against his grazing palms and a slight triumphant smile curved his mouth, she knew she was helplessly lost again. For a young woman who had always been strongly self-disciplined, she was pathetically weak when it came to resisting Nick. Her love overwhelmed her misgivings, and she found it impossible to deny either him or herself the pleasures he had introduced to her—the special joy they had shared together last night.

Laine's eyes fluttered shut as Nick lowered his head. His hard mouth captured hers, exerting a slightly twisting pressure that sent a rushing thrill through her. With a little cry of total submission, she slipped her arms up around his shoulders and pressed her lips to his neck as he lowered her onto the bed again. As he lay down beside her, she turned eagerly to him, her hands undoing his belt and slipping his robe off his shoulders. She delighted in the touch that swept over her in intimate exploration, possessing what was so undeniably his. His caresses tormented her until she let him know with her sighs and gentle touches she was eager to accept him with a tremulous sigh of ecstasy. Only then did she feel complete. And despite the consequences and loneliness she knew she might have to face in the future, at the moment she knew she was exactly where she belonged—with him.

After that there was no turning back. Nick moved Laine's belongings into his room and she uttered no protest. A display of outraged innocence would have been ridiculous, and besides, she had made her decision. She knew she had to give him her love even if there was little hope that he might ever return her feelings. She was gloriously happy; her only regret was that the days and nights of her holiday were slipping by so unreasonably fast. By Saturday she longed to be able to make time stand still in this exclusive little world she and Nick were sharing. That was the prime reason she was somewhat disappointed when he informed her he had invited Walt and Joan Bennett for dinner Saturday night. Though she liked the couple, she couldn't forget how little vacation she had left, and she wanted to spend every moment alone with him. Then, realizing her reaction was typical of a woman in love for the first time in her life, she was able to chuckle wryly at herself and begin to look forward to becoming better acquainted with Nick's friends.

Laine's newfound anticipation was rewarded. Saturday evening was truly enjoyable. The Bennetts were witty and unpretentious, which helped make the lobster dinner Laine and Nick had prepared together a complete success. After the meal, while the men strolled out on the deck, the two women made coffee to go with the raspberry torte Laine had baked. Chatting about their shared interests, they placed cutlery and china cups and saucers on a red and black Chinese enameled tray. Then as Laine was cutting generous portions of the torte, Joan suddenly ceased talking. The silence lengthened noticeably. Glancing curiously up from her task, Laine found the other woman watching her speculatively.

"Oh, dear, I didn't mean to be staring," Joan apologized, then gave Laine a mischievous grin. "But I was just wondering if you know you're the talk of the island these days?"

"Me? You must be kidding! I'm being talked about because I'm spending my vacation with Nick? Surely that doesn't shock anyone? I imagine he's had women staying here before."

"Oh, certainly, he has," Joan readily admitted with a dismissive toss of one hand. "No one's shocked because you're here, dear. We islanders aren't as provincial as that. The reason you're a favorite topic of conversation is that you're so different from the other young women Nick's had visit him here. And of course he treats you so differently that it's obvious to all of us that you must be someone special to him."

"I'm afraid I don't understand what you mean," Laine said weakly, a tiny perplexed frown knitting her brow.

122

"Why do you think he treats me differently from the way he's always treated previous . . . er, guests?"

"I don't just think it; I know it for a fact," Joan corrected as she took cream from the refrigerator and poured it into the cream pitcher. "You see, though Walt and I have known Nick for years, he's never gone out of his way to introduce the women who stayed here to his friends. Oh, I don't mean that he tried to hide them—if we bumped into him in the village or dropped by here, he happily introduced us. But he never seemed to care whether they met anyone or not. You're different, though. He brought you to our party and he invited Walt and me over for tonight. And I understand the Fredericks were here for a few days after you arrived."

"I still don't understand the significance," Laine confessed, rearranging the items on the tray to make room for the dessert plates. "I mean, simply because Nick chose to do a bit of socializing during this vacation doesn't necessarily mean I'm special to him."

"Maybe you didn't know that Nick hasn't been seriously involved with anyone in years. During his midtwenties there were some long-term relationships, but then his career skyrocketed and he never seemed to want to make time for a woman in his life." Joan smiled fondly. "Actually, I'm always telling him he's not the marrying kind, but since I've met you . . . well, I wonder."

"You're overestimating his feelings for me," Laine murmured, wishing she could believe in Joan's romantic notions but unable to. A regretful smile played over her lips as she shook her head. "I imagine you'll soon see that I'm gone out of his life and as forgotten as his other women are."

"I hope not." She paused. "You're really in love with him, aren't you?"

"I didn't realize I was so transparent."

"Probably only to another woman—women know how to read the signs," Joan said with a comforting smile. She hesitated a moment, then added, "I guess I could be wrong, but I think I've seen glimpses of those signs in Nick too. I'm certain he's very fond of you. And to tell you the truth, Laine, I think he's often lonely. He needs a woman like you."

"He might not agree with that," Laine reminded her, lifting her shoulders in a resigned shrug. "Actually, you were probably right all along—he's not the marrying kind. Who knows, maybe he's introducing me to all his friends because he's tired of being alone with me. Maybe he invited you and Walt tonight because he's bored."

Joan laughed. "Oh, I'm sure you know Nick better than that. Believe me, if you bored him, you wouldn't be here right now. Very likely, he would have asked you to leave. He can be blunt on occasion."

Lifting her eyes heavenward, Laine grimaced comically. "Tell me about it."

Their conversation was halted abruptly when Nick strode into the kitchen, but he seemed not to notice the sudden, rather guilty, silence. With a wry smile he glanced at the tray Laine was preparing, then looked up at her. "I'm sure Walt would never try to rush his hostess, but he can't seem to think about anything except the delicious dessert you promised him. So if you could bring it out soon, we might manage to stave off his near starvation. At least until his midnight snack."

"That man," Joan said, shaking her head, though her expression was lovingly indulgent. "He can eat as often and as much as he wants and never gain an ounce. It's so unfair. If I take one bite of any kind of dessert, I immediately gain five pounds. I'm serious; that's really true."

Laughing with Nick at the blatant exaggeration, Laine finished with the tray, then she and Joan preceded Nick as he carried it out to the deck. It was a moonless night, but the sky was star-filled and Nick had provided added illumination by switching on a couple of the post lamps on the perimeter of the deck. After dessert was finished and Laine had won Walt's rave reviews for her baking expertise, conversation continued, but at times Laine's thoughts were elsewhere. While she and Nick shared the lawn settee opposite the one where the Bennetts sat, she relaxed beneath the pressure of Nick's arm around her shoulders and was content as his fingertips idly brushed the smooth skin of her upper arm. She felt the oddest sense of belonging with him, and sometimes, like now, their relationship seemed more comfortable than those of many married couples she'd seen. But she reminded herself firmly that she was only playing hostess in his house and that the situation was not permanent. Yet, she couldn't erase Joan's comments from her mind. What signs of being in love had she glimpsed in Nick? What were the signs that betrayed a man's feelings? Laine wasn't altogether sure she knew. Attentiveness? Nick was attentive. Tenderly considerate? He was that too. Passionate? He was certainly that. But then, Nick had displayed those qualities since the moment she had met him, and he certainly hadn't loved her then.

As he spoke beside her, she used the opportunity to gaze up at his face, soft blue eyes searching his clear-cut features as if she hoped to find the answers to all her questions there. When she continued to look up at him even after he finished speaking, he noticed and glanced down at her with a slow indulgent smile then placed a teasing kiss on the tip of her small nose. Was that in any way a sign? she asked herself, unresisting as he drew her closer against him. And she felt a tiny bud of hope bloom inside her even as her mind warned in a haunting whisper that she was hoping for something she could never have.

The next day, Sunday, was different. It began well. After sleeping late, Laine and Nick had brunch, then took a long walk on the beach while Greta cavorted along beside them. When they returned about an hour later, they escaped the scorching rays of the midday sun by relaxing in the house. In the cool shutter-darkened great room, soft music played on the stereo, and when Laine started to join Nick on the sofa with a book, he pulled her down onto his lap instead. For a long time in a comfortable silence they simply held each other, his arms lightly around her, her own resting against his upper chest as she cupped the strong brown column of his throat in her hands. It was a sleepy kind of day, and Laine laid her head against his shoulder and responded drowsily when he occasionally covered her mouth with his, bestowing kisses that weren't preludes to intimacy, but self-complete and satisfying in themselves.

Laine had rarely felt so relaxed. The firm familiar lips that moved over hers with the lightness of a gentle breeze induced that sense of belonging again and she would have been content to remain in his arms this way forever. That wasn't to be, however. Suddenly, without warning, a forced interruptive cough shattered the peaceful silence. Laine opened her eyes and lifted her head as her father stepped between the sliding doors into the great room.

She took a swift sharp breath, hardly able to believe what she was seeing. Feeling as if someone had delivered a blow to her chest, she pressed a fist between her breasts and moved quickly yet with exceptional grace off Nick's lap to a place some distance from him on the sofa. Almost of their own volition, her hands went up to smooth her tousled sun-washed hair as she stared incredulously at Thornton Winthrop.

"Father! What are you doing here?" she nearly gasped,

then belatedly tried to disguise a comingling of dismay and shocked surprise.

"Nice to see you again, Thornton," Nick calmly interceded, rising to extend his right hand to the older man, mercifully giving Laine a few seconds to regain her composure. Surreptitiously, she took a few nerve-steadying breaths to help her recover from the shock of Thornton's sudden appearance. She wasn't upset that he had found her in Nick's arms—he should have expected that. What did upset her was that he had even come. It wasn't like him to seek her out, and that in itself made his motive suspect. She strongly suspected it was his desire for further information about the grant rather than concern for her that had brought him here. Unaware that her lips were pressed tightly together, she simply stared at her father as he took a seat in the chair across from the sofa. She saw him flick a cool gaze over her faded cut-off jeans and equally faded halter, and when he gave her a thin smile, she was incapable of returning it.

"Well, Laine, your tan gives you a nice healthy glow," Thornton commented at last, adjusting the collar of his short-sleeved knit shirt as if he didn't know what to do with one that didn't have a tie beneath it. At last, his hands dropped down to rest on the arms of the chair and he nodded as he continued to look at his daughter. "Yes, you look well. Didn't I tell you a vacation would do you good? It's amazing how revitalizing sunshine and fresh air and exercise can be." When neither she nor Nick had a response to such an obviously correct statement, Thornton attempted another smile. "Well, I was just out for a drive and decided I might as well come to St. Simons. Hope you don't mind my dropping in, Nick."

"Certainly not. You're welcome anytime," Nick replied, apparently not the least disconcerted by the transparency of the older man's excuse, or by the surprise visit.

Seated on the sofa again, he turned to smile gently at Laine. "Perhaps your father would like something cool to drink after his drive. It's a bit early, but it's a hot day. Why don't you make us both a whiskey sour." He turned back to Thornton. "I've discovered Laine makes a terrific whiskey sour. She even remembers to leave out those godawful cherries."

Though the compliment had been genuine, Thornton chuckled knowingly. "I see you've trained her right," he said with excessive jocularity. "Not all houseguests are willing to fetch and carry."

Though Laine tensed and was on the verge of making some retort until Nick caught her eye, his understanding smile coaxed one to her lips and she even managed to include her father in it. Within seconds she was grateful he had prevented her saying anything. Most of her adult life she had refused to let her father make her lose her temper. And she wasn't going to allow him to upset her unduly now, simply because he had arrived unexpectedly.

For the next thirty minutes or so Laine was on pins and needles. Every time her father opened his mouth, she expected him to mention the grant, and since the grant was such a source of friction between Nick and her, she wasn't exactly thrilled that her father would undoubtedly bring it up. Wishing he hadn't come, she sipped her white wine and said little. Sitting on the sofa, beside but not too close to Nick, her feet tucked up beside her on the cushion, she merely listened as the men discussed a variety of topics.

As it happened, it was Nick himself who brought up the subject of the grant, following a short lull in the conversation. Relaxed on the sofa, long tanned legs stretched out in front of him, he took a swallow of the amber liquid in the cut-glass tumbler. "Tell me, Thornton, have the auditors finished at Latham yet?"

The older man masked the flicker of disappointment in his expression almost immediately as he placed his glass on a coaster. "Actually, they finished Tuesday. I thought you might have their statement by now."

"They're to send it to my Atlanta office," Nick explained. "I imagine it will be there waiting when I return week after next. But I doubt I'll be able to examine it right away."

When her father only nodded, saying nothing, she felt a keen stab of compassion for him. She wished Nick could ease his worries right now but she knew Nick better than that. He was a thorough man, and after calling auditors in he would make no decision until he had seen their statement. He had no real way of knowing that Thornton Winthrop was an excellent administrator and that Latham College was an efficient, well-run institution. He could rely only on facts and figures, plus his own personal instincts. And all the evidence was not in yet. She couldn't help wishing, though, that for her father's sake she could snap her fingers and make the grant theirs.

About ten minutes later Thornton made excuses to leave. Rising to his feet, he shook Nick's hand again and turned to Laine. To her surprise, he put an arm around her and kissed her cheek. And although the brief, unaccustomed embrace had been somewhat clumsily executed, she smiled up at him after kissing him back. He simply nodded in response, not unusual for him. "Nick's right. You make a fine whiskey sour, Laine. A very refreshing drink for a hot day like this." He walked out onto the deck, then turned back for an instant. "You'll be home Sunday. Right?"

"Yes, Sunday," she called after him. "Good-bye, Father."

Then he was gone. Breathing a deep sigh, Laine walked back to the sofa where Nick had taken his seat again.

Sitting down, legs tucked up beside her, on the rug at his feet, she leaned her head against his knee. "I have to apologize for Father," she said softly. "I've never seen him this way. Usually he has incredible patience when a decision's being made that will affect Latham. But with this grant, he's too anxious to wait patiently."

"I'm surprised you didn't set his mind at ease," was Nick's icy response. "Why didn't you tell him you'd already sacrificed your virginity for the cause? That might have reassured him."

With the graceful swiftness of a gazelle, Laine sprang to her feet, but before she could take more than two steps, Nick caught her by the wrist, jerking her back down onto her knees on the rug before him. "Where do you think you're going?"

"Home," she retorted, trying in vain to twist her wrist free of a viselike grip. Resentment flushed her cheeks and flashed in her eyes, and she was nearly overcome with a sudden desire to flail at him with her fists. She didn't dare, and it wasn't only an inherent revulsion to violence that prevented her. Yet her defensive anger was unabated. In fact, it flared to impotent fury when he hauled her closer and leaned forward on the sofa until his breath was fanning her cheeks. "Let me go!" she exclaimed softly. "I want to leave! I'm sick and tired of your accusations and I won't stay here and listen to any more of them. If you can really believe I would . . ."

"The way you acted just now while he was here didn't help me believe otherwise," Nick interrupted, his voice deceptively calm. As aqua eyes, blazing with defiance, met his frigid green stare, his hands slipped up to grip her upper arms, fingers pressing into her flesh. His expression hardened. "You should have seen yourself, Laine. You were jumpy as a cat. As if you were afraid he might scold you for not playing your part. Why let him intimidate you when you know he must realize exactly what kind of relationship you and I now have? He's not stupid. He has to know we're sharing a bed."

"Father's blinded himself to the truth in this entire situation. He's probably convinced himself I'm here 'fetching and carrying,' as he said, and simply being nice to you."

"Surely he knows you'd do much more than that in an attempt to please him?"

"But I *wouldn't!* You're absolutely wrong about that." Her voice fell, her tone became less angry, more urgent. "Nick, for God's sake, why do you go on and on about my relationship with Father? I'm not obsessed with pleasing him. In fact, I know I usually can't, so I certainly wouldn't sacrifice anything in an attempt."

"I know you'd like to believe that, but . . ."

"If what I'm saying isn't true, then why did Father come here today to learn something about the grant? Why should he have had to? Surely, as soon as I'd traded myself for the million dollars, wouldn't I have called him and told him he had nothing to worry about?" She was nearly shouting at him now, but she didn't care. "If I'm so anxious for his approval, then why didn't I call him? Why is he still concerned about the grant? And there's something else." Her tone dropped to a lower, more reasonable level. "*He* might believe I can influence your decision, but *I* don't. I don't think anything or anyone could keep you from making the decision you thought was truly right." For an instant she imagined she saw something like confusion flit over his lean dark face, but then it vanished and she was no longer certain what she had seen. Anger drained away, leaving her empty and miserable. Unable to look directly at him any longer, she riveted her gaze on smooth hard shoulders and neck, wishing she dared tell him she loved him. But it all seemed so hopeless. No matter how she tried, she couldn't convince him that she wasn't prostituting herself for the grant. And since he believed she was capable of doing that, there was little chance he could ever feel real affection and respect for her, much less love. Yet if there was even the slightest chance . . . She lifted her head to gaze up at him, unaware that her darkening eyes mirrored all her confusion, her vulnerability.

"Dammit, Laine, you're driving me crazy," he groaned, pulling her up into the tightening circle of strong arms, crushing her against him. His lips took the parted softness of hers with savage force, then gentled with persuasive demand when she arched closer and wound her arms around his waist. "Temptress. Sweet little temptress," he whispered into the opening flower of her mouth. "You know how to make me forget everything, and I can never resist the temptation."

She couldn't resist either. His lips, plundering the sweetness of her mouth, were arousing passions in her that soon equaled his. But that was the way it was. Although he didn't trust her and she knew staying with him now would only sharpen the pain she'd feel when the relationship ended, they didn't seem able to walk away from each other. It was a fascination that wouldn't last forever, at least not for him, and Laine knew that. But simply being with him now made it far too easy for her to forget the way it would end.

CHAPTER EIGHT

The days slipped by too quickly. Dread mounted in Laine when she thought ahead to the coming week. She had no idea if she would ever see Nick again after their vacation ended. If their involvement had meant no more to him than a mere holiday fling . . . It made her feel almost physically ill to even consider that very real possibility. Since she had never been one to live only for the present, she also began to wonder if she would have regrets. Would she be terribly sorry she had given heart and soul for two brief weeks of happiness? Right now she regretted nothing. But right now she was still with Nick, she reminded herself as she lay beside him on the beach late Wednesday morning.

Propping on one elbow, she gazed down at him. He was asleep. His firmly carved lips were slightly parted and the thick fringe of his dark lashes lay against brown skin. She had to suppress a desire to brush back the lock of hair that fell forward across his forehead. Free to survey him as closely as she wanted, she allowed her gaze to drift over the broad muscular chest and flat abdomen, down along the wholly masculine lines of long powerful legs. She took a deep shuddering breath. She could hardly believe all that had happened in such a short space of time. Nick had awakened the most feverish desires in her, and she had responded to him with an abandon she would have never have believed herself capable of. How was she supposed to forget what they had shared? She didn't think she would ever forget one single moment of her time with him and could only hope her memories wouldn't become so much a part of her life that she would begin to live in the past. She did have a future. She really did, she repeatedly told herself. She might even meet another man she could love as much as she loved Nick. But she seriously doubted that, and as he stirred beside her on the blanket, she laid back down and hastily brushed away the fat teardrop that had been captured in her lower lashes. And when Nick lifted himself up onto his elbows and looked down at her, she smiled lazily at him, as if she, too, had been peacefully asleep.

It was during lunch that the phone call came. Nick was gone from the table almost fifteen minutes, and since Laine could hear only the deep rumble of his muffled voice from the study adjacent the great room, she had no idea what the call might be about. Her curiosity was piqued, however, and when Nick returned to the dining room somewhat later, she smiled questioningly.

"Laine, I'm sorry," he began ominously, both his expression and his tone grim. "I have to fly to Pittsburgh this afternoon for at least a couple of days."

Her heart seemed to plummet to her stomach and she clenched her hands together in her lap as her smile slowly faded. "I see," she finally managed to say, though it was devastating to know the end had come so early and so completely without warning. "Wh-what time do you have to leave?"

He was watching her closely. "As soon as possible. But I'll be flying up in my own plane, so I won't have to wait for an available commercial flight."

"Oh, I didn't know you had a plane," she said rather

woodenly, lacking anything better to say. "You didn't tell me that."

"No . . . I guess I just never thought of it. But that's not important now." Coming around the table, he crouched down beside her chair, reaching out to brush a tendril of sun-silvered hair back from her temple. "Laine, I'd like to take you with me, but I don't think that would be wise." He gave her an endearing smile. "You're far too intriguing, love, and I don't seem able to keep my mind, not to mention my hands, off you for very long. If I decide to accept this case, my client's going to need all the energy and concentration I can manage from the very beginning. He's been accused of more than one murder, and what he doesn't need is a lawyer whose attention's divided."

An answering smile tugged at the corners of her mouth. "I understand," she told him, and she did. Especially with such serious charges hanging over him, this client would need Nick's total commitment. Pushing her own disappointment aside, she slipped her hand into Nick's and moved her chair back to stand. "Come on. I'll help you pack. After you're on your way, I'll pack my own things and drive home before dark."

Dark narrowing eyes swept over her as he shook his head. "I expect you to stay here," he said, almost if it were more a command than a request. But as he cupped her face in his hands, the brushing strokes of his thumbs over her cheeks were gently coaxing. "I should only be gone a couple of days, and you're still on vacation. Why don't you just relax while I'm gone? Enjoy the beach. Play with Greta. You wouldn't feel uneasy being here alone, would you?"

"Oh, not at all." She moved one hand in an indecisive gesture, knowing it would be wise to leave. Yet she was so very tempted to remain. After only a few seconds emotion overcame logic and she nodded up at him. "Okay, I think I would like to stay."

Though he nodded and gave her a slight approving smile, she could see that his thoughts were drifting away—to the prospective client in Pittsburgh, she imagined. They talked little as she folded shirts neatly into his brown leather suitcase and he put two suits into a zippered travel bag. Then the packing was done and they walked from the bedroom, Laine's heart sinking little by little down to her stomach as she began to realize he would be gone a couple of days. She would miss him—there was no point in denying it. It was disconcerting to know she had become so accustomed to his company that she dreaded the prospect of time spent without him. It was a feeling she had to quickly lose; she knew that too. Next week she would be back at Latham, alone, and she had no assurance that she would see him often—or ever—after that. The mere thought sent a stab of pain through her heart. She hastily thrust it aside as she watched Nick lay the travel bag over the back of the sofa then walk into his study. He returned with a briefcase which he placed with his luggage.

Slender and lightly tanned, shapely in a light blue tank-top and cutoff jeans, Laine stood in front of him, looked down at her bare feet for an instant, then back up at him. It took all the effort she could muster to try to smile nonchalantly.

Nick's answering smile had a pensive quality to it. "I'll try to be back by Friday afternoon." He glanced at the thin gold watch on his wrist. "I'm going now."

She nodded. "Do you want me to drive you to the airport so you won't have to leave your car there?"

"That's all right. It'll be safe in the lot. I always leave it."

"This plane of yours . . . is it very small?"

"Six passenger. Why do you ask?"

"Oh, it's just that those little planes always look so fragile to me." Gazing up at him, nibbling her lower lip, and allowing a faint frown to touch her brow, she added impulsively, "You will be careful, won't you?"

An amused glimmer in his narrowed green eyes accompanied a now mischievous smile. "I didn't plan to do any barnstorming on the way."

"I didn't imagine you would," she replied pertly. "I just know that you're anxious to get to Pittsburgh, but don't forget to check the weather forecast and to file a flight plan."

"You sound like a mother," he accused lightly, reaching out with both hands to pull her to him, drawing her arms up around his neck. His lips sought the scented hollow beneath the delicate curve of her left ear as long strong fingers slipped through her hair. "But it's not mothering I want from you, Laine."

A shiver of delight trickled down her spine as the tip of his tongue probed sensitized skin, but she asked very seriously, "What do you want, Nick?"

"Much more than I can have right now," was his less serious answer. Tilting her chin up with his thumb, tightening his arm around her narrow waist, he brought her close against him and lowered his head. Firm demanding lips swiftly took the tender curve of hers. With a murmur, she stretched up on tiptoe, delighting in the hard line of his solid frame, to which her softer contours yielded. His kiss lengthened, deepened, scorching her with powerful intensity. He would release her mouth only to cover it with his again. And again . . . until the blazing flame of their mutual need threatened to consume them.

Curiously unsteady hands spanned her waist, and he put her away from him. As his gaze swept over her upturned face, green fires of desire glinted in his eyes. If only she could see love as well as desire there, she thought with sudden aching desperation. Then she thrust that futile thought aside to whisper with deliberate provocation, "Sure you wouldn't rather stay here with me?"

"Vixen," he whispered back, his slight smile a mystery as he released her and proceeded to gather up the gear for his trip. With his hands full, he effectively prevented himself from taking her in his arms again, but he did lean down to brush a lingering kiss of good-bye across her lips.

He left immediately. After carrying his briefcase to the Jaguar for him and waiting for him to slide in beneath the wheel, Laine watched the car disappear down the pebbled driveway. Hands in the pockets of her cutoffs, she stood there staring after him for several long moments. The island airport was only minutes away and she knew that probably within a half hour he would take off. Turning back toward the house, she kicked a sprinkling of sand against a clump of sea oats and sighed. She doubted if he would think about her at all while he was gone, but she was certain she would think almost constantly about him.

Thursday it rained all day. Laine read the morning away but by the time lunch had come and gone, a restlessness was gnawing at her. She could no longer concentrate on the pages of the book she held. Thinking back about the past ten days, though, she realized with some surprise that she had spent nearly every single minute of that time with Nick. Little wonder she missed him so terribly now. Putting her book aside, she looked down at Greta, who lay at her feet on the great room's area rug. Amazingly for a creature who loved to frolic in the ocean, the dog was excessively prissy when it came to rain. She had scratched at the sliding doors and gazed in at Laine with such a woebegone expression in her brown eyes that finally she had made it inside.

"At least I have you for company, don't I, girl," Laine said to Greta, then laughed wryly at herself when the dog cocked her head inquiringly to one side. "Are you wondering why I'm here and Nick isn't? Frankly, I'm beginning to wonder myself."

By Friday morning, though the sun did shine again, Laine's doubts had multiplied. Without Nick's reassuring presence, she was no longer so certain she should stay and await his return. She was in deep enough anyhow. Staying could possibly make the situation worse. If it could be made worse. . . . As it was she was tormented by thoughts of how completely happy she could be if only he loved her, and she knew she would only succeed in extending her misery by indulging in such wishful thinking.

Perhaps she should make the break now and go home while Nick was away. Or perhaps she should stay and take every second of happiness with him she could have. Bombarded with such conflicting alternatives, she sought escape by spending Friday morning in the village, browsing through the shops. Later, after lunching alone back at the house, she went for a swim, although she knew very well she was running out of time in making a decision about whether or not she'd stay. When Nick had called last night, he had told her he still planned to fly back to St. Simons Friday afternoon. If she decided to go but didn't get away before he arrived home, she knew all too well that she wouldn't go at all. He would only have to be a little persuasive to get her to stay with him. The flesh is weak and, increasingly, Laine's love for Nick overcame logic. Her heart was ruling her head.

"Fools rush in," she murmured to her reflection in the bedroom mirror as she combed her freshly washed hair after her swim. Uncertainty clouded the blue eyes that looked back at her, and when she noticed the barely discernible downcurving of her mouth, which seemed to give her such an air of vulnerability, she uttered an oath beneath her breath. Willing herself to make her decision

139

within ten seconds, she made it. She would stay. Next week would be soon enough to begin the painful process of accepting that Nick didn't love her.

When Nick phoned a half hour later to say he would be delayed in Pittsburgh until Saturday afternoon, Laine concealed her intense disappointment. But after their brief conversation ended, she moaned softly. The days she had left to try to gain Nick's love were slipping so quickly away, and with that thought came the realization that she had always felt a foolish hope that somehow he would fall in love with her too. It was a hope she had tried fervently to deny, but now that she accepted its presence, she feared the heights to which a hopeful imagination might take her.

Then she was struck by a brilliant idea. To escape Nick's house and the foolish daydreams she might have there, she would drive home and make her father's dinner. Anything to occupy her mind, she thought, as she hurried to dress. Deciding to treat Greta by taking her along, she called the dog from the beach, wiped her damp sandy paws with a cloth, then led her out to the Omni.

In itself, the drive home was relaxing. Fresh air poured in the open windows, and Laine enjoyed Greta's reaction to the ride. Sitting erect and alert in the front passenger seat, ears perked, the dog watched the world stream by with great interest. Traffic was light. The trip which sometimes took thirty-five to forty minutes was completed in less than thirty. And Greta's curious interest was intensified when Laine let her out of the Omni and took her inside the Winthrop house.

Leaving the dog to her sniffing tour of this strange place with all its strange scents, Laine went into the kitchen to take stock. She found a package of lamb chops in the refrigerator, obviously her father's purchase for one of his week's solitary meals, and she wondered why he hadn't cooked them. Actually the refrigerator was too well stocked, as if he hadn't prepared many meals at all. Hadn't he been eating well? A twinge of conscience was immediately squelched. Her father was an adult, capable of cooking for himself. She couldn't allow herself to feel guilty if he hadn't eaten right simply because she had taken a well-deserved vacation.

Smiling as Greta wandered into the kitchen and then back out again, Laine began dinner. By six, when she expected her father home, everything was almost ready. With nothing left to do except put on the final touches, Laine went into the living room and was delighted to find a letter from Regina, a rare thing indeed. Curling up comfortably on the sofa, she soon discovered why her sister had addressed the envelope to her alone. Since Regina never discussed her romantic entanglements with her father, this letter wouldn't have been suitable reading material for him. In it, she described in glowing terms the newest man in her life, and as Laine read the impetuously scrawled lines, she wondered how long his appeal would last. The letter was long, and just as Laine was finishing the last page, she heard the front door open and her father come in. When he entered the living room, she looked up and smiled, despite the deep furrowing frown he was wearing.

"Why are you home so early?" he questioned sharply. "Did something go wrong? Did you and Nick . . ."

Interrupting hastily, she explained Nick's unexpected emergency, then saw quite clearly the visible relief that flooded her father's face. It was so obvious he had expected to hear she had done something to antagonize Nick that she felt a small surge of resentment. But it soon passed, and while Thornton sipped a drink, she returned to the kitchen.

She nearly jumped out of her skin when her father suddenly bellowed her name. Certain he must have fallen violently ill, she raced into the living room, only to find him cornered by the bar staring down at Greta, who was growling softly at him. Laine spoke a command, and the dog immediately relaxed her aggressive stance and stopped growling.

Jerking up his head, Thornton glared at his daughter. "What the devil is this . . . mastiff doing here?" he exclaimed heatedly. "Are you trying to give me heart failure? Why didn't you tell me there was a dog in the house?"

"She's been roaming around upstairs and I just forgot for a moment she was here," Laine told him, gesturing apologetically. "I'm sorry if she scared you. She's just never seen you, and I suppose she thought you were an intruder. But actually, Father, she's not large enough to be a mastiff."

"I don't care what she is. Remove her at once from this house," he snapped. "I can't imagine why she's here in the first place . . . unless . . . Good God! You haven't bought her, have you?"

Smiling wryly, Laine shook her head. "No, Father, I didn't buy her, but I did feel I should bring her with me this afternoon since I'm taking care of her for Nick."

The mere name brought about a change in countenance. Thornton's frown faded. "Oh, she belongs to Nick. Well, I see." He cleared his throat somewhat uncomfortably. "Then I guess you did have to bring her with you."

"Yes, I did," Laine said, leaving the room when her father actually decided to approach Greta and stroke her sleek head.

Fifteen minutes later dinner got off to a less than promising start. As Thornton was unfolding his napkin in his lap, he began talk about the grant, as if he thought she knew whether or not Nick had made a decision about it. And when she reminded him that Nick hadn't yet seen the auditor's report, he seemed to doubt she was telling the truth.

"Well, you must know something more than that," he said harshly. "Surely you and Nick talk about the grant?"

Calmly slipping her knife through a perfectly done chop, she shook her head. "Actually, the grant doesn't come up very often."

"Then what the devil are you doing on that island?"

"Having my vacation," she replied succinctly, looking at him with a spark of defiance in her eyes. "Remember, you were the one who insisted I go there and relax. I didn't realize you really meant for me to lobby constantly for the grant. That would have done no good, I assure you. Nick would have undoubtedly asked me to leave if I'd tried pressuring him into a decision. He's not a man to push, Father."

Having no answer for that, Thornton maintained a cool silence for the next several minutes. When he finally spoke again, it was only to tell Laine that she looked considerably neater than she had when he had visited the beach house Sunday. After one last disparaging comment about her cutoff jeans and halter, he was silent once more, this time for the remainder of the meal.

By the time dinner ended, Laine was ready and eager to return to St. Simons. Sheer restlessness had brought her home, and it had been a mistake to come. Her father, in his present crabby mood, was no one to spend a relaxing evening with. After cleaning up in the kitchen, Laine took her purse off the counter and walked into the living room. Greta, who had been sprawled out in a nap on the rug, sleepily raised her head.

"Yes, come on, girl," Laine called, then glanced at her father. "I'm going now."

Thornton lowered the newspaper he was reading to look over it at his daughter. "Very well," he answered with a nod. "Drive carefully." And when Laine simply smiled a good-bye and started out of the living room, he cleared his throat again.

She stopped and turned around to look at him. Obviously he had something more to say and she waited expectantly.

"Nick must trust you," he at last stated, watching her rather speculatively. "He's letting you stay at his house, even while he's away. That sounds good. The two of you are obviously developing a good friendship. Just don't forget how influential friends can be."

"Father, Nick wants more than friendship from me," she said quietly, though her patience was beginning to wear a bit thin. "I should think you'd be aware of that."

He smiled weakly. "Well, of course, I know that he sees you as an attractive young woman and that you think he's an attractive man. I imagine your relationship could develop into a romantic involvement, given time."

Laine stared at him disbelievingly for a second, then shook her head but made no reply. Any answer would have gone unheeded anyhow. Her father had simply closed his mind to the truth. Since he had practically thrown her into Nick's arms, he was apparently unwilling to recognize just how deeply she had become involved. As Nick had said, he wasn't a stupid man, but he had certainly stuck his head in the sand in this situation and Laine wasn't inclined to force the issue. Let him hide in his guiltless idealistic dreamworld for as long as he could.

After murmuring a final goodnight, Laine led Greta outside to the car. As she drove away from the house, she wearily pushed the sweep of hair back from her forehead. She had never realized before how tired her father made her feel. His steady nit-picking and vague disapproval didn't make for a very joyous homelife, and suddenly she had the keenest, sharpest need to be with Nick again.

144

Maybe he didn't love her, but at least he treated her like a truly valuable person.

Nick still hadn't returned, and it was early Saturday afternoon. To avoid considering he might be delayed yet another day, Laine decided to do the bulk of her packing now instead of postponing the chore until Sunday. In Nick's bedroom she stood for a moment gazing out the wide window through which moonlight had shone in on them that first night.

Dragging herself away from the disruptive memories, she went to the closet and began removing some of her clothes. It was as she was standing before the chest at the foot of the four poster bed, folding an ice blue sundress into her suitcase, that she was abruptly overcome by the eerie sensation that she was being watched. Spinning around, she found Nick standing in the doorway, observing her solemnly, and as her heart started beating errati-cally at the mere sight of him, he came into the room.

"You're back," she said unnecessarily, managing not to run and fling herself against him and show him how very glad she was. "I didn't hear you come in. I . . ."

"Why are you packing?" he asked flatly, stopping to flick back the sides of the tan suit jacket he wore and place lean hands on equally lean hips. "You weren't thinking of leaving today, were you?"

"I'm just packing what I can now instead of leaving it until tomorrow." Though his expression lightened some-what, she still could see fine lines of strain around his mouth and she took a step toward him. "You look tired, Nick."

One long stride brought him to her and he pulled her into his arms, close against hard warm strength. When her hands slipped up to cup his neck, he bent down to give her the gentlest of kisses, his firm lips playing lightly over the softness of her mouth. "Umm. That's much nicer than what I've been doing for the past two and a half days," he whispered only half teasingly, then stepped around her to lower himself into the easy chair by the bed. He drew her down onto his lap.

Delighted that he seemed to have missed her at least a little, she smiled at him, laying her hands on his shoulders, her fingers massaging the tensed muscles. "You obviously took that man on as a client. And obviously you expect it to be a difficult case."

"It usually is when the client's guilty," he stated with incredible calm, then shook his head in gentle admonition as her eyes widened. "Even the guilty are guaranteed a defense in this society, Laine."

"But I've being reading about the case in the newspaper," she protested softly. "And if he really committed murder, several of them in fact . . ."

"He's quite insane, doesn't even remember his crimes except under the influence of sodium pentathol."

"Even so, you can't want to help set him free!"

"You're precisely right—I don't want him to go free. But I don't want him to go to prison either. He's too uncontrollable for any place except a maximum security psychiatric facility. He'll probably never be cured—he's so deeply psychotic. But researchers might learn a great deal about what causes his particular illness. Maybe they'll learn enough to develop a treatment and there won't be as many senseless killings committed." Sighing, Nick raked his fingers through his hair. "It's always an uphill battle, trying to convince a jury that a defendant should be confined to a mental institution rather than a prison, especially if he's been judged competent to stand trial. I guess too many sick people have been released from psychiatric facilities, and I can understand their fear. But I don't believe this man would ever be released. He's so obviously mad. Pathetic and repulsive at the same time."

For the first time Laine truly recognized what different worlds she and Nick lived in. Hers was a world peopled by innocent children while his was often peopled with society's most troubled outcasts. He shared some of the bleakest moments in people's lives, and she was seeing now how some of those experiences could drain him. He had needed someone to talk to today and she was so very glad he had chosen her to confide in.

"Thank you for telling me about the case," she said, tenderly touching her fingertips against his cheek. "I know what you've said is confidential and I'll never repeat a word of it."

"It never occurred to me that you might," he murmured, tightening his arms around her until she was lying against his chest. One large hand clasped the back of her head, holding her fast. His mouth descended with all-consuming need onto hers while his free hand swept over her from head to toe, caressingly exploring every enticing feminine curve.

Breathless from the overpowering desire conveyed by his mouth, hands, and body, Laine dragged her lips away from the taking strength of his. Sensing a barely leashed passion more intense than she had ever known in him, she felt a fluttering of fear in the pit of her stomach. She caught his face in her hands to resist another kiss. "You had a long flight," she breathed. "Can't I get you a drink or something to eat? Aren't you hungry?"

"Only for you. God, I *need* you, Laine," he groaned, overcoming her ineffectual resistance with ease. His lips were on hers again, hard, possessive, seeking surrender. Too aroused to unbutton her blouse, he jerked it open, and two or three buttons popped off to land with a click on the hardwood floor. Laine's slight fear became sudden delight and she reveled in the insistent need conveyed by the hardening line of his body. As he swiftly removed her lacy wisp of bra and lowered his head to close his mouth around the rose-tipped peak of one breast then the other, the moist pulling pressure he exerted sent wild desire coursing through her. With a soft moan, she urged his mouth to hers again. Her hands slipped reluctantly from him when he stood with her in his arms then deposited her on his bed. She watched him shed his clothes through heavy-lidded eyes. And when he came down onto the bed beside her, she moved eager stroking hands over his broad smooth back as he slipped his fingers beneath the waistband of her shorts and undid the snap.

The overwhelming urgency of his lovemaking struck a responsive chord in her. She held nothing back. With each slow rousing thrust of their lovemaking, she wrapped herself closer to him, her lips clinging to his, whispering his name over and over between tremulous sighs of pleasure. He possessed her totally, body, soul, and mind, and his hands on her slender curved body exercised that right of possession. He took her spiraling upward to the piercing peak of ecstasy then joined her there until the warming waves of satisfied desire rippled through both of them. Together they slipped down into intense contentment and lay close together, arms embracing, legs entangled as their breathing slowed.

Her eyes fluttered open to meet the smoldering fires warming his, and when he smiled gently, she pressed a kiss in the hollow just beneath his jaw.

"I missed you, Nick," she allowed herself to confess softly. "I'm glad you're back."

"That's good to hear," he murmured, stroking her delightfully tumbled hair. "If you missed me, then it'll be

148

easy for you to say yes when I tell you I want you to move in here. You will come live with me, won't you, Laine?"

She could only gasp, and when he laughed softly, almost indulgently, at her reaction, she stared at him in stunned surprise.

CHAPTER NINE

"Oh, Nick, be serious," she finally said. Composure regained, she forced a light little laugh, hoping he didn't notice it was patently false. "I know you. You're too independent to want any woman to live with you."

"I didn't ask 'any' woman. I asked you. I like having you here, Laine," he said in a tender, sincere voice. "And since you seem to be happy here with me, I see no reason why we shouldn't try living together."

Try living together. How very casual he made it sound. And as Laine had to accept that he was being serious, an inner chill radiated over her entire body and seemed to seep into her very bones. Without even realizing it, he could hurt her so easily, and she was hurt now as the foolish hopes she had harbored crumbled to dust. His affection for her had not become love. With this proposition of his, he as much as said that he found her temporarily intriguing but that he didn't really expect his interest in her to last. They could play house together until they tired of each other, then go their separate ways. Maybe he really could do it that way, but she couldn't. Already her emotions were in tatters, but she couldn't tell him that truth. Instead, she turned up her lips in a little smile, hoping her cheeks didn't look as frozen and stiff as they felt.

"I . . . don't see how I could live here," she said slowly,

willing herself to relax again in his arms. "I'd have to drive to Latham and back every day, and that's a lot of miles."

"I've considered that. It would be somewhat inconvenient, but I hoped you might think it was worth it to live at the beach," he murmured beguilingly, trailing little kisses along her jaw, closer and closer to her mouth. "Hmmm. Laine, wouldn't you like to live at the beach . . . with me?"

She could easily have cried. She longed to accept what he offered. Yet it wasn't enough without his love. By swallowing repeatedly, she eased the strangling restriction in her throat, and sheer will power enabled her to endure the burning behind her eyes without allowing the tears to flow. When his lips ceased wandering to cover her own, parting their softness with a gentle, irresistible demand, she kissed him back fully, betrayed by her body. Nick knew only too well how to arouse her, awaken a burning, insatiable need in her. Only he knew that one secret spot on the nape of her neck beneath silken hair where the mere brushing touch of his lips was like fire dancing over her sensitized skin. He knew everything about her except that she loved him, and she could not sacrifice the tattered remnants of her pride by confessing that she did. She wouldn't, *couldn't* set herself up for such devastating rejection. Somehow, then, she had to give him practical excuses for not coming to live with him so he would never know the truth—that she was terrified of being too happy with him for a few short weeks or even months only to lose everything in the end when he became bored with their relationship. She had gambled once and lost. She couldn't gamble again.

Knowing she needed to play her chosen role convincingly, she laughed softly and escaped Nick's caressing lips by pushing gently at his chest. "Stop, Nick, you're not playing fair," she chided teasingly, veiling the hurt in her eyes by lowering her lashes. "How can I think sensibly with you kissing me like that?" She paused and ran her tongue over her lips. "I do wonder if it would be very wise of me to move in here when you're really not home all the time yourself."

"It's always seemed silly to rush home to an empty house. Now, if you were here . . ." Cupping her face in both his hands, he kissed the tip of her nose. "But I know you want to think about this before making a decision. Why don't we just talk about it again next weekend? I'll probably be in Pittsburgh most of the week, but I'll drive to Latham Friday night or Saturday morning. You can tell me what you've decided then."

Laine jumped at the proffered reprieve, knowing she could hardly bear to make the break with him at this very moment. She needed the next week to shore up her defenses, to bolster her courage, because some dreadful instinct told her that when she declined his invitation to live with him, everything between them would immediately end. Nodding, she gazed up at him and tried to smile. "All right, I'll tell you next weekend. Why don't I make you something to eat? After that long flight, you have to be hungry."

To her relief, he admitted he was, and after tangling her fingers compulsively in his dark hair and urging his mouth down to hers for a kiss that was, for her, almost a goodbye, she got up. Draping his terry robe over her shoulders, she went into the adjoining bathroom for a shower, leaving him half asleep in the bed.

Laine's time left with Nick seemed to pass in the twinkling of an eye. Sunday morning sped into Sunday afternoon, and then it was time for her to start the drive back to the Latham campus. After stowing her luggage in the back of the Omni, Nick opened the door for her to slip in beneath the steering wheel, then closed the door behind her. As she was fumbling for her keys in her purse, he bent down from his considerable height, reached in through the open window, and took her small chin between thumb and forefinger, drawing her inexorably to him. He leaned his head inside the car to give her one final kiss. Unable to prevent her lips from clinging to the firm shape of his, she slipped her hands with some urgency over his arms, conveying a too obvious need to be closer to him.

"Laine, Laine . . ." he groaned, reluctantly releasing her mouth. Though his green eyes flared hotly, his smile was gentle. "Are you absolutely certain you have to leave tonight? Tomorrow morning . . ."

"I have to go now, Nick," she muttered thickly, thrusting the proper key into the ignition to switch on the engine. Afraid her voice would break revealingly if she tried to say any more, she simply gave him a rather tremulous smile that seemed more shy than sad. And lifting her hand in a hesitant wave, she gently pressed her foot to the accelerator and moved away from him. It was only when she was halfway along the drive, as she involuntarily looked up into the rearview mirror and saw Nick still standing in the same place watching her leave, that she allowed a soft tearless sob to escape her. If only he had said one word of love to her, everything could have been so very different.

By Friday evening, when Nick called Laine to tell her he would arrive at her house in about an hour, she had convinced herself she was ready to face him. During the whole long week since she had seen him, the push and pull of her emotions had practically made her numb to all feeling. Yet she had come to one irrefutable conclusion— she was more old-fashioned that she had ever considered herself to be. Too many times during the week her eyes had automatically sought her left hand and the ringless third finger began to take on great significance. In this new self-understanding, she realized that to truly find happiness in her love for Nick she needed to be married to him. Even if he could return the love she gave, that wouldn't be enough to persuade her merely to live with him. Now she knew she could never be content in such a casual nonbinding arrangement. She could never deliberately plan to just live with him.

The two weeks of her vacation had been different. She had gone to stay with him, believing other guests would be there and, in her naiveté, believing she could actually control her own desires and his. The intimacy they had shared had begun spontaneously, and only then had she recognized that what had happened had been inevitable from the beginning. But if she chose to live with him now, even if he could love her, she would be willingly settling for less than she needed. Her own sense of self-worth wouldn't permit her to do that.

"Something *isn't* always better than nothing, after all," she told her reflection in the vanity mirror Friday evening. Straightening the collar of her white sleeveless cotton blouse and smoothing her tan textured cotton skirt, she took a deep breath and touched amazingly steady hands to her hair when she heard the front doorbell ring.

She went downstairs. Mercifully, her father had let Nick in and then disappeared, so she didn't have to deal with him, too, when she first walked into the living room and saw Nick. Standing with his back to her at the French doors that opened onto the patio, he was looking outside at the gathering twilight. Tall, so endearingly masculine in casual khaki pants and a navy rugby-style shirt, he evoked disturbing memories of what they had had together and she was made overwhelmingly aware of what she would be losing when their relationship came to a close. Before her resolve could weaken, however, she walked farther into the room and softly called his name.

He turned to her, and the lines of weariness etched on his face were almost her undoing. Every fiber of her being ached as she longed to throw herself into his arms to tell him yes, she loved him and needed to be with him, no matter what the cost. Standing perfectly still, she said nothing. With two long strides, he met her, his arms sliding possessively around her waist as he pulled her hard against the lithe strength of his long body.

"It's been some long week, love," he murmured huskily, cupping her face in one large hand and lifting it to receive his kiss.

To be able to store one last happy memory, Laine responded with the eagerness he had taught her to feel. Her softly shaped mouth opened slightly and with the ever-increasing demanding pressure of his lips, physical pleasure, honed to a fine edge by emotional agony, shafted through her. She felt bereft when Nick released her mouth and his arms slipped from around her, but she managed a slight smile as he sat down on the sofa, pulling her down close to him.

"How's the case going?" she asked, compelled to touch with her fingertips the fine lines of strain beside his mouth. "You look so tired, Nick."

"It's nearly impossible to defend a client who doesn't really even understand what's going on around him. But I'll have to do it, since the court probably won't rule him incompetent to stand trial." He shrugged. "Well, I don't want to talk about that right now. Maybe later . . . How did your week go, Laine? Miss me?"

If only you knew how much, she wanted so badly to confess. Instead, she forced a smile and looked away from his intense, warm gaze. "I guess I thought about you once or twice," she teased, laughing out loud when his face fell.

155

"Once or twice!" He was only pretending to be so outrageously hurt, she could tell. But did she see some genuine sign of vulnerability there as well? She lifted her hand and stroked his cheek. "Once or twice every minute," she assured him quietly. He relaxed again, holding her tight, and they both laughed, Laine amazed that she could actually seem so happy and relaxed when she was hurting so badly inside.

After telling about what had been a rather uneventful week, she fell silent, tensed for the question that was inevitably coming. And when Nick actually did ask her if she had made a decision, she almost felt relieved.

Nodding, she made herself look at him directly. "I've thought about it a lot," she said very softly but clearly. "And I've decided I can't live with you."

"I thought you were going to take some convincing," he announced, showing no surprise whatsoever at her answer. Taking one small hand in both his, he played lazily with her fingertips. "Laine, I think I understand some of your misgivings. Even though couples who live together aren't unusual these days, you do live in a rather close-knit community on this campus and I imagine gossip is rife. And I can't really blame you for not wanting to be the subject of some of that gossip, but . . ."

"Oh, but that's not it at all," she protested earnestly. "I admit I don't care to be gossiped about. But I don't actually let myself worry too much about what people like Dulcie Jacobs say. That's not why I'm saying no."

"Suppose you tell me why then."

"It's . . . well, I just can't say yes."

"That's a very poor answer, Laine," he persisted, a tiny frown beginning to etch his brow. "Now, try telling me exactly why you think you can't say yes."

"Oh, different reasons," she evaded. Wondering how long she would have to endure this torturing inquisition,

156

she balled her free hand into a fist in her lap. Her heartbeat slowed to the dull heavy thudding of despair as she detected a growing coolness frost his eyes and harden his expression. She hated lying to him, yet pride made her do it and she knew she had to play out the farce to the end. She forced her shoulders up in a vague shrug. "One reason is that moving into your house just doesn't seem . . . well, feasible."

"Or maybe you simply aren't willing to make that kind of commitment. Is that the problem, Laine?"

A bitter little laugh rose in her throat but she suppressed it. How ironic it was that he thought living together constituted a commitment while she believed that sort of arrangement indicated a lack of one. More certain than ever that such differing philosophies could never be reconciled, she averted her gaze as she murmured, "I'm not unwilling to make a *real* committment. I just . . ."

"We're good for each other, Laine. You know that," he interrupted, his voice lowering, taking on a hard impatient edge as his fingers pressed down against the delicate bones of her hand. "Don't you think that what we had together was special, Laine?"

Not special enough, she cried out inwardly, threatened by emotions that were on the verge of slipping out of control. Yet her expression remained deceptively placid as she overcame the growing need to snatch her hand from his and run from the room. And pride intervened again, enabling her to appear calm as she answered his question, "What we had *was* special, Nick, at least to me. But I still can't come live with you."

His jaw tensed. Piercing green eyes raked over her mercilessly. "Don't say you *can't* as if some malevolent force were holding you back. Say what you really mean—that you *won't* live with me."

"All right, I *won't* then." She winced slightly with his

abrupt release of her hand. Her gaze swept over the hard planes of his face, reading impatience in every line, and that impatience simply seemed another indication that his feelings for her didn't run very deep. Anguish darkened her eyes but she veiled them swiftly with the fringe of her lashes as she added almost in a whisper, "I'm sorry I've made you angry, Nick."

"I'm not angry. Disappointed, yes," he replied coldly, standing to look down on her while a grim smile moved his lips. "You have proved to be a disappointment, Laine. I thought maybe you'd finally be able to cut yourself loose from Thornton and from your own irrational need to try to please him. But you haven't done that, have you? He's the reason you've made this decision. What it comes right down to, Laine, is that you can't bear the thought of displeasing your father."

His theory was so far from the truth that Laine was literally struck speechless for several moments. Then all the old denials she had given Nick so often before raged forth in her again, seeking a voice. But before she could open her mouth to utter a protest, he seemed to have taken her silence as affirmation of his theory and was halfway across the room. She started to call his name but he suddenly turned around and his brown face was such a daunting mask of cold indifference that she could only stare at him mutely.

"Tell your father I expect to make a decision about the grant within the next few weeks," he stated, his words clipped, precise. "Good-bye, Laine."

He was gone and she heard the soft firm click of the front door closing before she fell back limply on the sofa and raised trembling fingers to the throbbing ache in her temples. Her thoughts were in such a confused jumble that she was just coming to the full awareness of what she had done tonight when her father inopportunely entered the living room.

"Why did Nick leave so early?" he questioned her sharply, arms folded across his chest. "I saw him leave and he certainly looked less than pleased about something. For God's sake, I hope you haven't managed to antagonize him somehow, Laine. If Latham doesn't receive that grant . . ."

"To hell with the grant, Father," she said, turning on him with utter rage and disgust in her tone. She stood and walked past him into the foyer. "Right now, I don't give a damn about the grant and I don't give a damn about anything you have to say. I'm sick and tired of your constant faultfinding anyway. . . . Excuse me. I'm going to bed."

And she left him staring after her in stunned disbelief. Yet, even that gave her no satisfaction. In the privacy of her room, she made a soft almost wounded sound as she lay down across her bed. Drawing her knees up against her breasts, she wrapped her arms round her legs and closed her burning eyes to the soft glow of the vanity lamp.

So, she had achieved her objective tonight. She had made the break with Nick now so he couldn't do it later, yet the spreading emptiness that ached inside her told her that hers had been a Pyrrhic victory at best. Maybe she had salvaged her pride, but pride was cold comfort when everything else was irretrievably lost.

CHAPTER TEN

Marge leaned in at the open doorway to Laine's office, a hopeful smile on her pleasant face. "Are you terrifically busy right now?" she inquired. "I've been wanting to talk to you, but if it's not convenient, I can come back later."

"Now's fine," Laine mumbled around the paper clip pressed between her lips while she shuffled several file folders into a neat stack on her desk. Taking a somewhat impatient swipe back at the golden hair that tumbled across her forehead, she sat back in her aged swivel chair and gave Marge a genuine but almost restless smile. "Don't tell me another one of our little overimaginative charges has gone home and told his parents we spank them with 'great big old sticks' here."

Marge chuckled wryly. "Not this time. Hopefully, only Myron Benson has that wild an imagination, so maybe that little fib won't be told on us again. And actually, I don't want to discuss anything school-related. What I have to say is personal this time." Her smile fading to nonexistence, she studiously examined her fingernails, then glanced back up at Laine uncertainly. "Honey," she said gently, "I really don't think you can go on much longer this way. You're never still a minute. If there's no work to do, you manufacture it, and after two weeks of pushing yourself to the limit of physical endurance, you're beginning to look more than tired. I'm so concerned about you."

"Oh, you shouldn't be. I'm fine. Really, Marge," Laine responded, lifting one hand in a dismissive gesture. She began to tap the eraser end of a pencil lightly against her desk pad. "I'm just in one of those restless moods. We all seem to go through it on occasion. Maybe I shouldn't have taken a long vacation. I seemed to come back with all this bottled-up energy. Two weeks of relaxation can be an overdose, I guess."

"Don't try to pretend with me, honey. I know something's wrong." Marge leaned forward in her chair, across the desk, concern written on her face. "You're not trying so hard to keep yourself busy because you've had too much relaxation. I don't think your vacation was as calm and uneventful as you say. Something happened while you were away, and I noticed a difference in you the moment you got back. The first week you worked, you were *so* preoccupied, and now for the past two weeks you've been burning the candle at both ends. Laine, you simply cannot take over the chores of the entire staff. Can't you tell me what's bothering you? Maybe it would help to talk. And besides, you must know by now that you can't escape problems by working yourself half to death."

"You're exaggerating. I'm not working myself half to death." Laine shook her head and smiled. "I just feel like keeping busy lately. And I don't know why you imagine anything happened to me on my vacation. It really *was* pretty uneventful."

"You went to St. Simons, right?"

"Um-hmm. It's really a nice place, isn't it? Are you and Joe taking the kids there this year?"

"We haven't decided for sure yet. And you're not going to succeed in trying to change the subject," Marge announced sternly. "I want you to talk to me, Laine. I imagine you might need to talk, since it's very doubtful that two weeks spent with Nick Brannon could have possibly been uneventful."

"So you know I was with Nick." Laine shook her head in amazement. "How on earth did you hear about that? Surely, Father didn't go around advertising the fact that I was spending my vacation as Nick's house guest."

"Your father didn't have to say anything. A friend of Dulcie Jacobs's lives on St. Simons. She called Dulcie and mentioned you were there. And you know Dulcie. *That* tidbit was all over the campus in three seconds flat."

"Two seconds if she really put her heart into it," Laine added wryly, unaware that her rather resigned little smile added a touch of vulnerability to her features. "But I don't really care who knows where I spent my vacation. I do wish you'd tell me, though, why you think I was different when I came back to work again."

"Falling in love makes people a bit different," Marge said gently, understanding warming her eyes. "And being badly hurt or disillusioned makes them different, too, in another way." Reaching over, she gave the younger woman's arm a comforting squeeze. "You can deny it all you like, but you've experienced both the love and the hurt since you met Nick Brannon. You're in love with him, aren't you?"

Wearily massaging one shoulder with her hand, Laine nodded. "Unfortunately, that doesn't mean the feeling is mutual."

"Are you still seeing him?" Marge asked, then answered her own question. "You aren't, are you?"

"No."

"I'm so sorry, dear," Marge murmured, her own eyes filling with commiserative tears though Laine's remained dry, even virtually unclouded. "I know you're going through a painful time. Nothing is quite so miserable as loving someone who doesn't love you back."

"Ah, what the heck, I'll survive," Laine responded, though her attempted flippancy wasn't exactly an award-winning performance. Looking down, she picked a nonexistent piece of lint from the skirt of her cotton-blend grass green dress, as she added almost inaudibly, "After all, other people survive unhappy love affairs. I'm not the first person this has happened to, and I certainly won't be the last. And I'll get through it . . . sooner or later."

"You really will, Laine," Marge assured her softly. "I promise you that you really will."

"And I know that . . . at least in my head." Laine's right hand moved over the general area of her heart. "But there's something else inside me that makes me afraid that loving Nick will always hurt just as much as it does now."

"It's too soon yet to put it all behind you. You'll need more time." Marge's expression brightened somewhat. "But why are we talking about this in the gloomiest possible terms? You and Nick *could* work out your problems and be very happy together."

Laine shook her head. "Nick's not willing to make a permanent commitment, and I've discovered I couldn't be really happy with anything else."

Sighing, Marge regarded Laine intently. "What about your father?" she asked at last after some hesitation. "Does he realize how upset you are about all this?"

"Does Father ever realize anything about me?" Laine countered, only the slight tightening of her lips betraying a newly developing resentment. "He's surely noticed how quiet I've been since my vacation, but he's never bothered to ask me why."

"I can't say I'm surprised. That's why I hoped you'd talk to me, Laine. Everyone needs somebody to confide in. Your mother and I were close friends, you know, and . . ." Marge paused a second, her gentle smile conveying affection. "Well, I just wanted you to know how fond I am of you."

A suspicious dewiness glimmered in Laine's eyes. For three weeks now she had held tears at bay, but Marge's genuine concern could easily have brought on the deluge had not Laine refused to give in to overwrought emotions. When her chin began to wobble slightly, she clenched her teeth together to stop it. "Thank you, Marge," she finally said, her voice strained. "I guess I did need to talk. I've been feeling a bit lonely lately."

Marge got up and hurried around the desk to slip her arm around Laine's shoulders. She drew her head against her ample bosom to briefly stroke her hair. "Nick Brannon must be a fool," she announced with protective vehemence. "He'd be damned lucky to have you. If he doesn't know that, then maybe you're better off without him."

"Maybe," Laine murmured, though she didn't sound very convinced. When Marge released her, she rested back in her chair and smiled gratefully at the older woman. "I do feel a little better now."

"Any time you want to talk, I'm here," Marge assured her as she headed toward the door. "Be sure you remember to come see me the next time you're tempted to become a workaholic. In fact, don't you think you should go home now? It's well after six."

"I'm going in just a second," Laine promised, then straightened in her chair to call to Marge as she stepped out into the hallway. "Wait. Are you and Joe still planning to leave for Atlanta this evening? Do you want me to take care of Jasper?"

"If you don't mind." Marge grimaced rather sheepishly. "And besides feeding him, could you go over to the house about nine at night to let him in? That cat will keep the neighbors up all night with his howling if he's left out. I'd hate for someone to wring his neck while we're gone."

"I'm sure that wouldn't put Jasper in a pleasant mood either," Laine quipped. "I'll be happy to bring him in at night and put him out in the mornings. It's no problem."

After Marge expressed her appreciation, she went on down the hall. Ten minutes later Laine locked the door to her office and started home. Walking briskly—a leisurely pace induced too many disturbing thoughts—she arrived at her father's house in less than five minutes, and when she went inside, she was startled by a sudden squeal of delight that came from upstairs.

"Laine, you're late! Where have you been? I've almost bored myself to tears, waiting the past two hours for you to come home," Regina chattered as she flew lightly down the stairs, her platinum hair streaming out like a silken curtain behind her. Casually elegant in a cream linen suit accented by a scarlet silk blouse, she was a vision as usual. Her loveliness was only enhanced by the perfect smile that appeared on perfectly shaped lips as she saw Laine's astonished expression. Gliding across the foyer, she hugged her younger sister briefly; then, aiming in the vicinity of Laine's cheek, kissed the air somewhere beside Laine's ear.

Knowing Regina hated to smudge her lipstick, Laine paid no attention to the deliberate miss. She was far too glad to see her sister. Regina's antics would keep her mind off Nick's desertion for the next day or two at least. "Oh, I'm so glad you're here," she said sincerely, smiling as her sister beamed down at her from her perfect model's height. "But why didn't you call and say you were coming? This is such a surprise."

"Father certainly was surprised when I stopped by his office earlier," Regina said, laughing lightly. "Then, of course, he had to scold me for not getting home more often."

Laine nodded knowingly. "He *does* miss seeing you."

"Umm. Well, I'm just *so* busy I can't get away."

"Maybe," Laine suggested, "you could invite him up to New York to visit you?" And get him off my back for a while, her mind added silently, much to her dismay. Until that moment, she hadn't fully realized how discontented living with her father was making her feel. Shaking her head, as if to clear her thoughts, she looked hopefully at Regina. "Do you think you could ask him? I know he'd love to spend his vacation with you."

"Well, I guess I *could*. But . . ." Regina vacillated with a slight wrinkling of her perfect nose, "I'm not sure it would be a good idea for him to visit me. I'm always so busy." She dismissed the entire subject with a flick of one wrist. "Oh, we'll talk about that later. Right now, let's go upstairs and catch up."

Agreeable, Laine walked with Regina up to the guest bedroom, which had been hers when she had still lived at home. Pointedly ignoring the thought that Nick had once slept in the bed, Laine sat down on the edge while Regina posed on the vanity seat, long shapely legs tucked to one side, crossed at the ankle. Glancing around the beruffled room, she sighed dramatically. "Needs redecorating. Looks like a teen-ager still lives in here. And speaking of redecorating, when's Father going to do something about that stuffy old office of his?"

"Oh, it's not all that stuffy," Laine disagreed with a laugh, amused by Regina's ability to disguise even a minor insult with gay lightheartedness. She was so outrageously vivacious that it was nearly impossible to be offended by anything she said. Yet, Laine did feel compelled to provide her with some financial truths. "Maybe you didn't know how tight money is on college campuses these days. I suppose Father would rather spend redecorating funds on something he considers more important, like lab equipment, say."

Examining the toe of one of her fashionable low-heeled snakeskin pumps, Regina nodded. "Come to think of it, Father did mention some grant he's afraid Latham isn't going to get."

"Oh? What did he say about it?"

"Nothing much," Regina answered with a shrug. "He knows I can't pay attention when he talks about Latham." She dismissed that topic, too, with another flick of a wrist. "Oh, thanks for the postcard from St. Simons. Did you have a good vacation?"

"Fine," Laine murmured, almost tempted to confide in her sister. It had helped some this evening to talk to Marge, so maybe telling Regina would ease some of her inner tension too. She took a deep breath. "About St. Simons . . ."

"You know, that postcard nearly made me ask Joel— he's the man I wrote you about—to take me to St. Simons for a week," Regina interjected impetuously, obviously unaware of interrupting her sister. Her violet eyes clouded. "It's a good thing I dropped that idea. Joel turned out to be dull as dishwater."

For the next half hour, Regina recounted the faults of the man who's many virtues she had just extolled in a letter only a few weeks ago. There was little reason for Laine to listen intently. She had heard the story so many times before. Regina would meet a man, fall in love with his utter perfection and, on occasion, even allow him to move into her expensive apartment with her. Then within weeks, two or three months at the most, the rose-colored glasses would come off and she'd see her "perfect love" as not so perfect after all. There would be much weeping and gnashing of teeth for a week or so, then she'd recover and start the entire process all over again.

It was weeping and gnashing time now. Laine nodded now and then as the emotional narrative went on, but naturally her thoughts drifted to Nick. And she was glad she had talked to Marge about him earlier because Regina didn't seem inclined to let her get a word in edgewise now. Besides, she wasn't at all certain her older sister could really understand the depth of her feelings for Nick. Regina only became superficially involved with men while Laine's involvement with Nick had been far more emotionally ensnaring. And she did feel ensnared, trapped by her love for him, and she could only hope that Marge was right—time would bring relief.

When Regina began to wind down some time later, she at last claimed Laine's full attention by pensively tapping a perfectly manicured finger against a perfectly hollowed cheek. "You know, I'm going to tell you a secret," she announced solemnly. "Joel, when he was moving out, told me . . . that I rely too much on my looks in my relationships. He said . . . I don't give much. And I've been wondering if he might be right. My relationships with men *never* last long. Maybe Father's pampered me too long. To tell the truth, he's spoiled me so much that I feel kind of uncomfortable around him. I feel like I have to *look* perfect or he won't like me. And of course, I've always hated the way he picks on you. Really, it's very silly. *You're* more like Mother in personality. I just look more like she did."

"Well, don't worry about how he treats me. I don't," Laine said, stretching the truth a bit. She paused a moment, listened, heard noises downstairs. "Speaking of Father, though, that's him now. We'd better go down so he can talk to you before dinner. What would you like to have to eat?"

"You don't cook on Fridays," Regina protested. "I remember."

"In your honor, O Famous New York Model, I'll make an exception," Laine quipped, feeling more relaxed than she had in weeks as she and Regina went down together.

The feeling didn't last. When Laine and her older sister stepped into the living room, Laine stopped short, her heart leaping up in her throat when she saw Nick standing by the bar with her father. Her breath caught audibly and the blood drained from her face with astonishing speed, inducing a horrid dizziness. Yet, when Nick turned and his narrowing gaze swept slowly over her, she fought to appear serene, forgetting how awful she felt, how wonderful it was to see him.

CHAPTER ELEVEN

"Girls! I was about to come up for you," Thornton proclaimed jovially as he turned and saw his daughters enter the room. Excitement fairly danced over unusually stern features and he actually beamed at Laine. "Nick's come to see you, but he also brought excellent news. Latham's been awarded the Winston grant."

Laine sent Nick a relieved and grateful smile but he never received it because Regina's squeal of delight drew his eyes automatically to her. From that moment on Regina set out to monopolize his attention by being her most captivating self. Laine was actually glad her sister was there. Seeing Nick again so unexpectedly had tied her stomach in knots, but Regina's nonstop amusing chatter helped her relax somewhat. Her gaze involuntarily moved to Nick every minute or so, however, and if he happened to be glancing at her, too, her heartbeat would accelerate to an unbelievable rate.

What was he doing there? she asked herself repeatedly. Her father had said he came to see her. But why? Had he merely told her father that to be polite? Maybe he had really only come about the grant. Yet, he could have phoned about that. Perplexing questions without answers chased themselves round and round in her mind until she was hardly able to pay attention to the conversation going on around her. Sitting on the sofa across from Nick's chair, trying not to appear the least bit tense, she pretended to listen to the others but only really did when she heard Nick mention he'd taken a room for the night in the local motel because he was driving on to Savannah in the morning.

"No need for you to stay in that sterile motel," Thornton spoke up. "We'd be happy to have you use our guest room."

Regina's laughter was almost a giggle. "Father, you've forgotten something—me! I'm in the guest room. Remember?" She cut her eyes coquettishly at Nick. "Of course, if Mr. Brannon wants to share the room with me, I think I just might consider it."

Her sister's audacity made Laine smile, but when her father actually laughed, she looked at him incredulously, astounded he found Regina's remark amusing. If Laine had ever made such a blatant remark, he would have gone right through the roof.

Nick was smiling, too, even as he shook his head. "A fascinating proposition, Regina, but under the circumstances, I imagine Thornton wants to rescind his invitation."

"I think I do," Thornton agreed, still chuckling. "But I'll offer compensation. You told me you were going to call on your old friend Jenny and her husband tonight, Regina. Why don't the four of you go to that nice little bistro, Pierre's, a couple of miles up the road? They have a great French cuisine there, Nick."

The suggestion stunned Laine. She could hardly believe she had heard correctly and was only barely aware of Regina's enthusiastic response to Thornton's idea. Determined to show no emotion, she consciously set her expression into the blandest look she could manage and simply stared at her father, resentment building within her. *What was wrong with him?* How could he even think of suggesting Regina go out with Nick when he himself had said Nick was there to see *her*? Breathing suspended, Laine sat waiting for Nick to remind Thornton of that fact. When he didn't, she knew she would never say anything herself, even if her life depended on it. Pride drew the line there. If Nick was too dazzled by Regina to remember he had come to see Laine, then he could just go to the devil. Yet when Nick calmly agreed to the night out with Regina without even a glance at Laine, she was appalled by the wave of intense pain that swept over her. She felt so betrayed. Riveting her gaze on her animated sister to avoid looking at Nick, she sat silent, misery welling up inside her.

Because Regina always put plan into action with little delay, she and Nick left the house almost immediately. Watching her sister smile up at him and tuck her hand into the crook of his arm, Laine winced, her anguish becoming a stiletto of piercing jealousy stabbing her chest. At that moment she almost hated her father for making her jealous of her own sister, and when she looked at him and saw his satisfied smile as the front door closed behind Regina and Nick, resentments, dormant too long, erupted to flow hotly through her veins. Perspiration gathered in the hollow at the base of her throat. Her cheeks burned. She continued to stare furiously at Thornton when he turned his head to face her.

"Well, Laine, what are we having for dinner?" he foolishly asked, then belatedly realized his error. "Oh, that's right. It's Friday and you don't cook. So I'll have to fend for myself, I guess."

Seething in outrage, she rose slowly to her feet. "You'll be fending for yourself every night soon, Father," she announced icily, her voice low and steady, "because as soon as I can get a faculty apartment or even a place in Brunswick, I'm leaving this house."

"What the devil are you talking about?" he asked impatiently. "What's wrong with you?"

"What's wrong with *me*!" Laine shouted, shaking her head disgustedly. "A better question is, what's wrong with *you*? How can you be so insensitive? How could you suggest Nick take Regina out when you must know by now how much he means to . . . How could you do that to me? You said he came here to see me. Don't you think I wanted to know why?"

"Well, uh, I guess that just didn't occur to me," Thornton replied, somewhat flustered, tugging at the knot of his tie. "I simply thought Nick and your sister might enjoy each other's company. I had no idea it would upset you if I suggested they go out."

"And I suppose it's never occurred to you that I actually have feelings," Laine persisted, her voice deadly quiet. Hugging her arms tight across her breasts, she surveyed her father with something akin to contempt. The expression that incongruously hardened her delicate features conveyed provoked rebelliousness, and gone forever was the patient acceptance of the past. A grim smile touched her lips but did nothing to soften the defiant spark in her eyes. She shook her head again. "What is it with you, Father? Haven't you even noticed how quiet I've been since my vacation ended? Didn't you see how upset I was when Nick left here angry that night two weeks ago? Didn't you begin to suspect that, while you were trying to use me as a bribe to get the grant, I was becoming more and more involved with Nick?"

"How was I to know you'd become infatuated with him?" Thornton blustered, shifting uncomfortably in his chair. "Besides, aren't you making mountains out of molehills? In a couple of weeks, you'll forget all about Nick."

"I rather doubt that. Maybe I'm weird or something, but I think I'm likely to remember my first lover," Laine stated bluntly, finding some small measure of satisfaction in her father's rasping intake of breath. His face flushed as he snapped up straight in his chair and she pressed on relentlessly. "Why so shocked, Father? You practically handed me to Nick on a silver platter. You were so obsessed with trying to get that grant you were willing to use me as bait. Now that Nick's given you what you want, though, you decided he deserved a better prize than me. So you handed him Regina."

"I didn't *hand* him Regina and I didn't use you as bait!" Thornton protested vehemently, raking his fingers through his hair. "I did ask you to be nice to him. But, good God, I didn't expect you to . . ."

"Oh, I'm not that big a ninny, Father," Laine interrupted curtly. "What I allowed to happen certainly wasn't for your benefit. As I tried to tell you, Nick could never be influenced anyhow. But nothing changes the fact that you nearly threw me into his arms and then didn't even notice I had fallen in love with him. And what you did tonight was the final straw. I can't live here any more. You'd better start looking for a housekeeper."

"Come, now, Laine, let's not be hasty," Thornton muttered, getting to his feet to gesture uncertainly. "I see now how upset you are, but after all, this is only a slight misunderstanding."

"There's no misunderstanding," she answered flatly, emotions spent and only cold resolve remaining. "In fact, I think I'm finally understanding things for the first time. The problem is and has always been *your* attitude toward me. Frankly, I no longer have the patience to ignore your insensitivity. My mind is made up. In fact, I'm not spending the night here. I'm going to Marge's to feed Jasper and I'll just stay there in her spare room until I've made other arrangements. I'm sure she won't mind."

"Laine, don't exaggerate this situation," Thornton argued, watching her as if she had been transformed into some strange, wild creature right before his very eyes. "You only have to feed the cat. You don't need to stay with him all night."

"Sorry to be so blunt, but at the moment I prefer Jasper's company to yours." With that, Laine marched out of the living room and up the stairs, where she tossed a nightgown, her toothbrush, and a few other assorted necessities into a tote bag. When she swept back down the steps a minute or so later and saw her father awaiting her in the foyer, she pressed her lips together, in no mood to hear another word from him. Ignoring the slight, beseeching movement of one of his hands, she stepped past him and out the front door, without even a backward glance as he called after her.

Marge's house was two streets away, and Laine cut through lawns to get there in a hurry. Delayed reaction was setting in, and her composure was beginning to fray along the edges. All she wanted was some time to hide herself away from the world and everybody in it. After searching for Marge's key in her purse, she let herself in and tossed her belongings onto a deacon's bench in the hallway. She went through the kitchen to the back door and opened it. Jasper, apparently on the point of starvation, was clinging to the screen as if he had been glued there, and the sight was so unexpectedly funny that Laine began to laugh out loud. Softly at first, then more and more uncontrollably, until the sound nearly became a sob before she at last managed to control it.

The numbness that had mercifully descended on her earlier was wearing off fast now. The aching heaviness in her chest became so oppressive she felt almost ill, and the tightness in her throat made even swallowing difficult. After spooning the famished Jasper's dinner from a small can into his dish, Laine started wandering through the house, too restless to sit down. As the hours dragged by, her thoughts became more and more distressing. She could see Regina and Nick together in her mind, and her imagination ran wild. She knew her sister. A man as attractive and intelligent as Nick could easily have her on cloud nine in a matter of minutes. And he, as most men did, had obviously found her irresistible. Laine knew all too well what that could mean. Their evening together could end in a passionate interlude in his motel room. Attractive men were Regina's weakness and an aggressive suitor like Nick could probably make her forget she had just met him.

Agonized by the thought of the man she loved and her own sister making love, she moaned softly, stopping in the doorway of Marge's den to lean her head wearily against the jamb. She tried to convince herself that Nick wasn't the kind of man who could go from one sister's bed to another's, yet . . . how well did she really know him? She had also believed he felt some affection for her, but if he did, it hadn't prevented him from going out with Regina tonight. Maybe he felt nothing at all for her then. Maybe he didn't care if he hurt her.

Seeking even the most superficial comfort, Laine took a long steaming bath. Afterward, she felt physically less tense, and when she had slipped on her nightgown, she immediately went to bed, curling up in a protective little ball beneath a light cover. In the darkness of Marge's guest room, however, the events of the evening clamored in her mind again and suddenly, without warning, a soft sob escaped her, then another. Tears began to flow. She couldn't stop them. Turning her face into her pillow, she cried for hours until, exhausted, she slipped into a dreamless sleep. It was the necessary emotional release she had battled against far too long.

* * *

With morning a semblance of composure returned. Laine awoke about seven, emotionally stronger despite a lingering physical weariness. Though thoughts of Nick still hurt and she knew they would for quite some time, she also knew what she had to do to take some of the edge off her pain. Last night she had laid out all her resentment at her father's feet. It was Nick's turn today. She might not be as candid in expressing her feelings to him, but she knew, to maintain her own self-respect, she must at least tell him he had been very inconsiderate, leaving with Regina when he had supposedly come to see her. Tired of having her strings pulled by her father for years and by Nick for weeks, she was now determined to cut herself loose from both of them.

Laine quickly washed her face and brushed her teeth, then put on her comfortable faded denim wraparound dress. She briskly brushed her hair until it shimmered like burnished gold and she pinched some color into slightly pale cheeks. In the kitchen a moment later, she started coffee perking and had a piece of buttered toast. It tasted so surprisingly delicious, she decided to have another. She felt very calm, almost eager to face Nick with what she had to say to him. It would be like an exorcism, one that might not bring real happiness right away but would at least be a new beginning. She had always considered herself an independent person, fully capable of controlling her own life, and this morning she was going to prove she was to Nick. Finishing her impromptu breakfast, she quickly washed the few dishes she had used, put Jasper out, and left Marge's to walk back to her father's house where her car was. Happily, Thornton didn't appear while she got into the Omni and started the engine.

Less than ten minutes later, she arrived at Nick's motel, spotted the Jaguar, and breathed a sigh of relief. Although it was early yet, only a few minutes past eight, she had been afraid he had already checked out. But he was here. She parked her car beside his and got out before she could even think of hesitating. Going to the lobby around the corner, she was told by the desk clerk the number of the room Nick was in, verifying her assumption that he'd parked almost directly in front of it. She retraced her steps, paused a moment before Nick's door, and unnecessarily smoothed her hair. The niggling little fear that she might find Regina with Nick dragged at her stomach, but she made herself dismiss it. Regina never stayed out all night when she was home for a visit.

Laine knocked on the door, then had no time even to take a deep breath before Nick opened it. Shirtless, his bared chest bronze, he stood barefoot on the threshold, dark trousers slung low on lean hips. His half-dressed state evoked a flood of disturbing memories, but she allowed none of her thoughts to be mirrored in her face. Her expression remained as unreadable as his.

"Morning, Nick," she began lightly, her smile no more than polite as she pulled her collar away from her neck. "My, it's hot already, isn't it? And muggy. I imagine we're in for a thunderstorm."

He glanced upward at the darkening sky. "Looks that way," he agreed, then turned sideways, indicating she should enter his room. "Come in, Laine. It's much cooler in here."

Wondering why he didn't seem at all surprised by her visit, she stepped inside. Though she tried to do it discreetly, her eyes immediately sought the bed and she breathed a silent sigh of relief when she saw that the sheets were only rumpled on one side and only one pillow bore an indentation. She looked back at Nick and found him surveying her closely, narrowed green eyes darkly mysterious. Shifting her straw purse from one hand to the other, she gave him another bland smile.

"I didn't get a chance to tell you last night but I've been reading about your Pittsburgh case in the paper," she said. "I'm sorry the judge decided to rule that your client's competent to stand trial."

Nick shrugged. "It was the ruling we expected." Dropping his hands from his hips, he stepped closer to Laine, close enough to brush fingertips over the faint violet crescents that lay beneath her eyes. "You look a little tired, Laine," he said softly. "What's wrong? Didn't you sleep well last night?"

"I slept fine, thank you," she lied, turning away from him to stare out the window. "I just haven't been feeling really well lately."

"Tell me what's wrong, Laine," he whispered roughly, moving behind her, sliding his arms around her waist. Long lean fingers spread open over her abdomen. "Are you pregnant?"

"Is that why you wanted to see me last night?" she asked, bitterly amused by his "concern." She tried to push his hands away but was foiled in the attempt as he turned her swiftly around to face him, imprisoning her in the circle of his arms. She ignored the compelling warmth that emanated from the body so close to her own and looked up at him, a rather mocking smile still lingering on her lips. "Is that why you came to tell father about the grant? Because you also wanted to ask if I'm pregnant?"

A muscle worked in his tautened jaw. "Just answer the question, please."

"I'm not on a witness stand. Don't play the attorney with me," she said coolly, with a slight outthrusting of her chin. "Besides, you didn't seem that anxious last night to ask if I'm pregnant. The need to find out certainly didn't stop you from going out with Regina."

Impatience glinted in his eyes. His hand around her

waist tightened and he shook her lightly. "For God's sake, tell me whether you're pregnant or not."

"I'm not. Most definitely not," she snapped back, straining against his arms, too aware of his superior physical strength. He seemed to tower above her, his very broadness blocking the light from the lamp behind him. Yet wariness was overwhelmed by some reckless perversity that drove her on, forced her to add tauntingly, "Are you happy now? Can you go home, relieved that all the loose ends are tied and you don't have to worry about a possible paternity suit that might hurt your career? Or did you find Regina so perfectly enchanting that you're going to stay around while she's in town?"

His darkly slashed brows lifted. "That sounds like jealousy, Laine," he murmured, a sardonic smile curving his hard lips. "Are you jealous because I went out with your sister last night?"

"What you do is no concern of mine," she answered primly but her newfound rebellion flashed in her eyes. "But let me tell you something. Nobody's ever going to treat me the way you did last night and not hear something from me, not you, not my father, not anybody. It was unbelievably rude of him to suggest you go out with Regina when he knew you had supposedly come to see me. And it was even ruder of you to agree. So, now that you know what I think of your lack of manners, I have nothing more to say." With an abrupt violent twist of her body, she freed herself from him. "I'm going now."

"I think not," he drawled, catching her arms again before she could take a step toward the door. She struggled to push his hands away, but he jerked her against him with such force that her breath was expelled from her lungs with a gasp. Gripping her chin between thumb and forefinger with little gentleness, he tilted back her head. The piercing hardness of his eyes impaled her, challenged the defiant spark in her own. "If you were so incensed by your father's suggestion, why didn't you speak up last night?"

"I expected you to say something. After all, you had said you were there to see me."

"Maybe you just didn't want to antagonize 'Father,' " Nick ground out, the contours of his face hardening, conveying ruthlessness. "I was hoping you'd finally find the courage to defy him. He gave you the perfect opportunity last night with his idiotic suggestion, but you simply sat there, Laine, and took it, as always."

"I took nothing. I'm moving out of his house and I told him so. He's never had any consideration for my feelings and . . . neither have you. Well, this is the end. He went too far last night and so did you, by going out with Regina."

"You goaded me into going out with her," Nick countered, his deep voice gruff. "You sat there as if you didn't give a damn whether I took her out or not, so I did."

"You really must think I'm simpleminded if you expect me to believe that," Laine said with a sarcastic twisting of her lips. "Don't you think I know men can't resist Regina? She's so beautiful, so . . . so *perfect.*"

"No, not perfect, Laine," Nick whispered, his hands on her suddenly gentling as his eyes swept with searching intensity over her upturned face. "Regina is pretty; she vivacious. But she's not perfect. Frankly, she impresses me as a young woman who merely skims over the surface of life. I'm sorry to insult your sister, but she's a shallow woman, Laine. After only an hour with her, I was bored. Needless to say, I took her home long before midnight."

"I don't believe that," Laine said flatly. "I know men think Regina is so sexy . . ."

"Sex isn't everything."

"It was all you ever wanted from me," she softly accused, her eyes clouding to deep dark blue, revealing her inner vulnerability for the first time since her arrival. Reluctantly, she pressed her hands against his bare chest, closing her eyes as flesh burned flesh. "Let me go, Nick. You've used me enough."

"I've never used you, Laine," he muttered huskily, slipping his hands up her arms to rest them heavily on her shoulders. "I had to take what you gave."

"You seduced me."

"You wanted me to."

Laine shook her head. "Not if you only did it because you thought I'd let you for Father's benefit. You had to be using me. After all, you practically called me a prostitute more than once."

"There were times when I could have called you worse. That night after we made love the first time, then you asked about the grant, *whore* was the word that came to mind."

Laine gasped. Her eyes flew open at the same moment one hand shot upward almost of its own volition, her palm itching to make contact with his dark chiseled face. The slap was never delivered. Nick caught her wrist and effortlessly twisted her arm behind her back. He didn't hurt her, but he apparently recognized her desire to hurt him, and when she pushed at his chest with her free hand, then pressed her nails hard into warm firm flesh, he nearly smiled.

"So there is a tigress beneath that calm exterior," he said, his tone strangely triumphant. "I've known your passion and suspected you hid other volatile emotions. But do you realize this is the first time I've seen you really furious? Now I can believe you tore into your father like a little hellcat last night. And that was one of the things that always bothered me. No matter what he said or did, you never lost your temper. So I had to wonder if you'd go to any lengths to gain his approval. And you have always wanted his approval, haven't you, Laine?"

"Maybe I have and just wouldn't admit it to myself," she confessed, her face the perfect picture of bewilderment as she gazed up at Nick's. "But I would never have gone as far as you thought I would to try to please him. I would never have let you . . ."

"You gave yourself because you had to and I had to take what you gave," he said softly, halting her words with a fingertip against her lips. His hands encircled her waist and he smiled almost sheepishly. "I've spent hours awake every night for the last two weeks, remembering what we had together. And it wasn't just sex, Laine. I wasn't using you. I *had* to be with you and you had to be with me. It was necessary for us to share everything, even a bed, because we fell in love, Laine. At least, I did. Did you?"

"Oh, Nick, yes," she whispered thickly, tears filling her eyes. After he gently kissed away a fat crystalline droplet that caught in the lower fringe of her lashes, she nuzzled her face against his brown neck, breathing in the beloved masculine lime scent of his skin. Her softly shaped lips explored strong contouring tendons as she repeated, "Yes, yes, yes, I fell in love too."

"Then say it," he commanded hoarsely. "I want to hear you say it."

"I love you," she obeyed eagerly. "So much, Nick."

"And I love you. God, I need you," he groaned, burying his face in her scented hair. "I have to have you with me. At the beach house. In my bed. Laine, will you . . ."

"Oh, Nick don't, please," she whispered brokenly. "I still can't live with you. I know you won't understand, but if I moved in with you, I just wouldn't feel right about it. It would make what we have together seem . . . oh, I don't know . . . cheap. I'm just too old-fashioned, I guess. Much as I love you and need you, I can't live with you."

183

With an oddly secretive smile, he sat down on the edge of the bed and drew her down beside him. He clasped both her small hands between his, lifting them to brush gentle lips across her fingertips. "Laine, you misunderstand," he said. "I admit I was angry when you refused to move to the beach house, but only because I convinced myself you didn't want to leave your father. I've had time to think more clearly during the last two weeks and I couldn't forget how you responded to me. You were a virgin, and women don't remain virgins until they're twenty-four by accident. Other men must have wanted you as much as I do—as I've told you before, you're an intriguing mystery few men could resist. But you'd never had a lover until I made love to you. And your response wasn't pretense. I remembered how innocently eager you were, how giving."

"I was eager because I love you. I've never really been in love before," she whispered, smiling tremulously. "Believe me, Nick, I hardly thought of Latham College or that ridiculous grant those two weeks we were together. All I thought of was you; nothing mattered except the two of us."

"I began to hope you felt that way. And I started to realize that if you did love me, our living together wouldn't be enough for you. I made a mistake when I asked you to move in with me. It was a mistake I'm not repeating now."

"What do you mean?" she whispered, hope rising in her, hope she was still afraid to have. "You just said . . ."

"I said I need you in my life—in my house, in my bed. . . . And I do," he reiterated softly, reaching back to pick up something from behind the lamp on the bedside stand. He turned around to her again, his expression serious, his dark eyes searching as they scanned her face. "This time, I'm asking you to marry me."

As an oval diamond set in gold and platinum was slipped onto the proper finger of Laine's left hand, her heart seemed to stop for an instant then began a rapid thudding as a joy more intense than she had ever known surged through her. Her wide eyes darted from Nick's face to the ring then back to him again and she whispered rather disbelievingly, "But you're not the marrying kind; you said . . ."

"Laine, what if I tell you that I've discovered my life is ridiculously empty without you?" he asked, spanning her waist with coaxing, caressing hands. "You're right—I had no desire to ever marry. My life can be very hectic; sometimes I receive threats because of the clients I represent. But I'm hoping you can adjust to all that. The law is very demanding, and I love it. I didn't think I could love any woman as much, but you've changed my mind. Laine, we belong together. Say you'll marry me, Laine, right away, the first of the week if possible. Say yes now."

"How could I say no?" she murmured huskily, love she no longer had to hide glowing like warm embers in her eyes. "You've always been able to persuade me to do anything you want. And since I want nothing more than to be your wife . . ."

"Tears again, Laine?" he questioned tenderly as her voice faltered. "I'd never seen you angry until today, and I'd never seen you cry."

"I learned how to cry again last night," she confessed, brushing her hands over the broad expanse of his bare muscular chest. "Oh, Nick, I've been so lonely without you. I'd never been so lonely in my life."

"Thank God you came here today," he said roughly, his impassioned gaze sweeping over her. "After last night when you let me leave with Regina without a word, I wasn't sure I'd been right to believe you cared."

"And if I hadn't come today . . ."

"I might have been forced to kidnap you some dark night," he teased, inexorably pulling her to him. His lips trailed fire over her cheeks. His breath was warm against creamy smooth skin. "How would you like to be kidnapped by me?"

"I think I'd like it very much. As long as there's no ransom," she murmured. "I'd like to think you wouldn't take any amount of money for me . . ."

"Because you're a priceless treasure to me, Laine," he finished for her. "You are, you know. You're real and warm and so giving. You give everything, Laine. And I love you too much to live without you now."

Laine's lips parted for his kiss, the first of many. When thunder began rumbling in the sky and fat drops of rain fell on the asphalt outside the dimly lit room, she was enfolded tightly in strong secure arms and her mouth was an opening flower beneath the coaxing pressure of his. Their kisses lengthened, became more langourously intense but were not enough. While the rain showered down, Nick undid the tie that closed her dress. He took it off; he then removed the last remaining barriers of her clothing. His eyes adored her. His hands glided over every contouring sweep of her slender bare body as if he were reclaiming by touch what had always been his.

After helping Nick undress completely, with a loving touch Laine lifted her arms to drape them across his shoulders. Her legs tangled with his, and as she felt the familiar roughness of his thighs against the smoother texture of hers, her soft breathless sigh signaled total surrender.

Yet as Nick moved her beneath him, his hands beneath her hips to arch her upward to receive him, the merging of their bodies brought a keener satisfaction than it ever had before. This time was different; it was her first time knowing he truly loved her. This time, not only did she belong to him—he belonged to her. And she whispered his name as the loving and pleasure they gave each other made them inseparably one. His passionate love filled her, and hers surrounded him. He was right—they did belong together. In each other, both of them found home.

LOOK FOR NEXT MONTH'S
CANDLELIGHT ECSTASY ROMANCES™

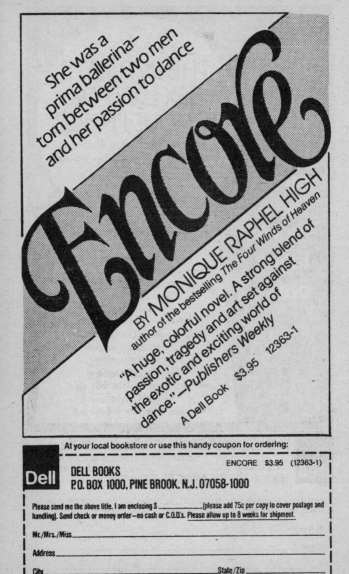

When You Want A Little More Than Romance—

Try A Candlelight Ecstasy!

The second volume in the spectacular Heiress series

The Cornish Heiress

by Roberta Gellis

bestselling author of
The English Heiress

Meg Devoran—by night the flame-haired smuggler, Red Meg. Hunted and lusted after by many, she was loved by one man alone...

Philip St. Eyre—his hunger for adventure led him on a desperate mission into the heart of Napoleon's France.

From midnight trysts in secret smugglers' caves to wild abandon in enemy lands, they pursued their entwined destinies to the end—seizing ecstasy, unforgettable adventure—and love.

A Dell Book   **$3.50**   **(11515-9)**
